18+, it contains graphic violence and gore. As always, there is a full list of TW and CW in my Bio's on all my Social Media pages and in the back of the book to avoid spoilers. Read at your own risk.**

!Warning!

This book is a Taboo-Horror book. So, expect grapic violence, gore and some straight up f*cked up shit. This is your warning that if those things do not interest you then you should turn back now. If you would like a full list of trigger warnings that is located at the back of the book to avoid spoilers.

The Maze

E.R. Hendricks

To all my girls who love a guy that is beyond saving, that is crazy and fully accepts it. And to all the girls that have a little crazy in them.

Blurb

These girls all have the same thing in common... they remind me of her.

And for that, they will suffer.

No one has ever made it out of my maze. I have designed it myself to be unbeatable, unpredictable, and unsurpassable.

So, why do we do it, you ask?

Well, isn't that obvious?

We enjoy watching the mice as they try to find the cheese that is their freedom.

The masters and they are the puppets.

But what do we do when one of those puppets uses my maze to cut her strings?

Will we give her the freedom she so rightfully deserves?

Or will we keep her for ourselves...

**The Maze is a Taboo, MMF Horror Erotica Romance. It contains dark themes and is only suitable for

objects are larger than they appear. This is not exact, just a replica.

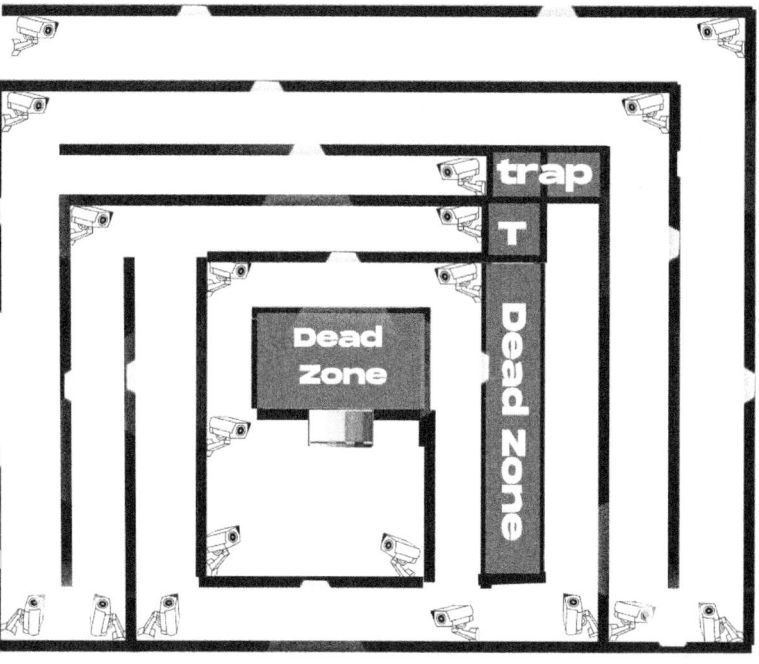

Chapter One

Lennox (Nox)

I slink back into the shadows, making sure I'm not seen. My eyes stay locked on the beauty before me. Her long blonde hair shines under the streetlights, highlighting her as she walks beneath them. I find myself searching for new details every time she steps back under the light, the dark teasing me and building my excitement. She steps under the next lamp and my eyes zero in on her tight ass as it flexes in her jeans as she walks.

Wanting to follow behind her but not be seen, I follow on the other side of the street; there are more broken lights on this side. I must admit, I'm surprised to find her walking alone in this type of neighborhood. At night no less. My guess is she has mace, they usually do, at least if they are smart. It's just a false sense of security. If a man wanted them, he'd get to them no matter what. I feel the right side of my lip rising on my face as I wonder if she will put up a struggle or not.

I hope she does.

I stay a good twenty or so yards behind her, making sure she never feels my presence. I'm dressed in all black to blend in better with the shadows. The fact that I'm tall and lean helps too, allowing me to move quickly and quietly. It's as if I was made for this. For stalking and hunting, the perfect predator.

My eyes track her every movement, my palms sweating as they fist at my sides. My pace picks up as the excitement works through me, my body anxious to make a move. This doesn't bode well for her. She doesn't even glance back once, she either lacks basic survival instincts or is just that dumb. Either way, she won't last long in my maze. The thought is almost enough to make me stop, but the off chance that she might surprise me keeps me moving forward. I also need to meet the quota, the games can't begin until I have enough girls.

She takes a right and heads towards a somewhat nicer neighborhood and I know my window to move is closing. I step from the shadows gradually getting closer.

"Excuse me, Miss?" I say once I'm close enough for her to hear. My voice is gentle and kind, if not a bit deep. But that's unavoidable.

She whips around quickly, her eyes widening as she spots me walking under a streetlight. I give a soft smile, making myself appear less threatening. I am very aware that to the majority of the population, I am what's considered conventionally attractive. With my chocolate brown hair and my slightly stubbled strong jaw and sharp cheekbones. Just another thing that makes me the perfect hunter; one you'd never expect.

"Yes?" She says after realizing that she's been silent for too long to be polite. Her eyes were too busy sliding up and down my body, stopping briefly on my crotch before working their way up to my face.

"I believe you dropped this. I found it about half a block away, on my way home from work." I say as I wave vaguely behind me. I hold a debit card out in my hand so she can see what I'm referring to. Her eyes go wide before she instinctively starts searching her person to verify that it is indeed hers. While her head is down and she's searching her pockets, I step forward and raise my other hand that holds a cloth covered in chloroform. I quickly press it to her mouth, she gasps in response; only taking more of the concoction deeper into her lungs before her legs slowly start to give out.

I step behind her, my eyes discreetly checking to make sure no one is watching. I drag her back into the dark alleyway. Her body twitches in an attempt to fight the inevitable. Let's hope she has more fight in her than this.

Once her body has gone completely limp, I lift her into my arms and walk the three blocks over to my La Voiture Noire. Granted, it's a bit flashy, but people are less likely to suspect someone worthy of committing a crime. Plus, the way I've propped her head on my shoulder looks more like she's cuddling with me than being kidnapped. I open the passenger side door and lower her into the seat before buckling her in.

I round the car before getting in and buckling myself in. The engine purrs as I turn it over, taking off in the direction of the warehouse. My life's work. I devoted years to making it everything I could have dreamed of and more, perfecting every square inch of it to fit my every whim. I drive leisurely into the countryside. I made sure the warehouse was not only inconspicuous in case anyone did happen to find it, but also made the odds of stumbling upon it slim to none. After driving the fifteen minutes outside of town and then down an unmarked road that says dead end, I take a few more turns until I'm driving up to the warehouse.

I press the cloth to her nose again, ensuring she won't wake up before it's time. Wouldn't want to ruin the surprise. I also check her pulse just to make sure she's not dead. It's happened before. I shake my head, remembering the wastefulness. But alas with mistakes comes growth.

I easily lift her lifeless body, carrying her into the warehouse. I know the maze so well I could go through it blindfolded. This helps since it's nearly pitch black as I take all the necessary turns till I reach the medium-sized center. It's set up like a room with minimal furniture, just things I've found at second-hand shops, random objects that I've placed around the room to serve a larger purpose; which they will find out later.

I smirk to myself, the anticipation and excitement building as the time inches closer. It's the only time I feel alive, during the games. I drop her unceremoniously onto the ground next to the rest of the girls before taking my leave.

There are thirteen girls in total that I've placed in my maze, each one looking just like the last. Their blonde hair shimmered in the harsh fluorescent lighting that hung just above the high walls, blocking their view beyond.

The muscles in my back flex, expanding and shifting as a sense of completeness, and rightness settles deep in my bones. The anticipation slowly building causes my heart to race and my mind to fizz. This is all I think about. Every day I am forced to wait between my games is like tearing off little chunks of my soul, ripping it away like shards of paper. Miniscule pieces ripped from my chest like confetti from a piñata. Finally, getting the girls here is like coming up for air after being shoved under the water. I gulp down those precious breaths, knowing that once this is done I'll be back underwater.

"Fuck!" I grunt as I adjust my hardening length in my black pants. The thought of it all turns me on like next to nothing else... nothing but *her*.

I exit the maze and make my way toward my upper office which is small and hovers over the maze, like box seats at an NBA game. I'm able to look over the maze and see most of the activity within it. The cameras that are hooked up to my computer allow me to view the rest. I sit down in my comfy office chair and start up my computers. There are six monitors in total, allowing me to get the best angle of all the action.

I lounge back in the chair, allowing everything to flicker on as I make myself comfortable. Within thirty minutes all the girls should be awake.

A smile rises to my lips as the first girl I brought in starts to stir. She lays there for around fifteen minutes, trying to clear her disorientation. Within that time, the second girl starts to groan and mumble incoherently. My pulse speeds up as more and more start to come too.

I chuckle to myself knowing how pissed Basien will be that he's missing this. Too bad because I'm not waiting, I've waited too long already. My pulse spikes with the excitement, soon, the games will begin...

Chapter Two

Lenah (Len-uh)

My head is pounding... How much did I drink last night? I reach over to grab my phone off the nightstand to check the time. My hand comes up empty, only cold, rough concrete greets me. My head lifts lazily, my body seeming to move slower than my mind is commanding it to. Internally I'm freaking out, but my body is moving at the rate of a snail and no matter how much I try to force myself to move faster, it won't. I grunt, frustrated as I try to force myself into a seated position, unsuccessfully.

What the fuck is going on! Where am I, why can't I move? My stomach turns and for a moment I think I might throw up. I would be shaking if I had control of my body.

It's then I hear the voices of others around me, they are distorted as if they are trying to talk through their hands.

"Je-cc-a?" My numb mouth fumbles as I roll over, calling out for my roommate.

"What the fuck! Where am I?" A panicked voice echoes my thoughts next to me and I realize I don't recognize that voice.

I force myself to sit up, my whole body aching as I start to gain back control. *What the fuck did I do last night?* I glance around the open space. Everything is blurry and I can't tell if it's my eyes or the hangover playing tricks on me. Scared voices sound out around me but I can't force more than gurgled sounds past my lips. My mouth is so dry it's like I ate sand all night. After a few moments of fighting my own body, I finally get my hands to my eyes to rub them out so I can properly assess my surroundings.

I clear the film from my eyes, only to be greeted by the eyes of about a dozen other girls just as groggy and freaked out as me.

"What's going on?" A short blonde girl next to me shouts. My brows furrow as I study the other girls. We all have varying shades of blonde hair. My heart rate spikes as I take in all the similarities between us. We each have our own styles and our faces look different, but I can't deny we all look like variations of each other. That can't be a good sign.

"Where are we?" My voice sounds grainy and rough like I've been crunching on rocks.

"No clue, but this is fucked up." I meet the eyes of the girl about ten feet from me, she's leaning up against the wall. She seems to be the most level-headed right now.

For the first time since I woke up... wherever the fuck I've woken up; I take in our surroundings more thoroughly. The walls are solid gray concrete, towering over us at what must be at least eighteen feet tall. I also notice there is only one exit to the room we are in with no door. I see paintings and other random objects hanging from the walls that don't seem to fit in the otherwise basement-esk looking room.

"What are we gonna do? How do we get out of here?" One of the girls whimpers as she sucks the snot back into her nose.

"We're gonna die. I can't die. I'm too young to die!" Another one babbles on. The energy shifts around us instantly, as if we are all sensing our impending doom at the same time. I shake my head, trying to deny those feelings, and instantly regret it as my head throbs so hard, I question whether it will explode.

"Shut the fuck up." The girl leaning against the wall states, calling the shots of our lost little tribe. "We aren't going to let ourselves go there!" She says sternly as her eyes meet each and every one of us. "We will figure out what's going on and we *will* get out of here. *All of us.*" She states like it's a well-known fact and a part of me... a small part that still holds on to hope, grasp on to that like it's the last dollar I own, and I need a meal. The other part can see we are super fucked.

"Okay then, Miss I have all the fuckin' answers. What the fuck are we going to do?" The babbler rebuttals, her tone irritated but I can see in her eyes she's begging for answers.

Our leader rolls her eyes, "Well, I can tell you, we aren't going to freak out because that's not going to accomplish shit." She huffs before using the wall to stand, her feet wobbling with the action. "Then we are going to go out, that exit." She finishes, pointing at the only opening out of this square box.

I clench and unclench my hands, trying to get circulation back to my limbs. I notice the other girls looking around warily but eager to get out of where we are. I can't say I blame them; I want to get the fuck out of here too.

After working my limbs enough to move, I force myself to stand with the rest of them. "Why do you think we are here, and has anyone else noticed we all look eerily similar?" I hedge, dragging myself closer to the wall before placing one hand against it for balance. Our 'leader' cringes slightly and I can tell she did notice that little tidbit. The other girls however seem to study each other more closely.

"Fuck!" one of them mumbles and I'm not sure who at this point.

"I have no clue why we are here, but I don't have any plans on sticking around to find out." Our leader says as she makes her way to the front of the cluster of girls. She conveniently ignores my other question as she takes a few steps out of the room before turning. "Come on, follow me." She waves us over before she turns to continue. A half second before I move to follow a wire snaps into place, slicing clear through her neck, severing it completely from her body. There's a long moment of complete silence as our brains try to catch up to what we've just witnessed before screams pierce my ears bouncing off all the concrete. Blood sprays from the arterial artery, covering the girls that were standing directly behind her. I watch in horror as her body stands entirely on its own for the space of three heartbeats before it falls to the ground. My eyes widen and I swallow down the bile rising in my throat. My mind racing as I slam my lids closed as if that will erase what I've just seen. It doesn't work, the vision replays before my closed lids, and I'm forced to open them again.

"Should we just go under the wire?" One of the girls says once the others have quieted enough to hear her

"Fuck no! What if there are more traps?" Another one answers. Fear has all of us frozen in place, not willing to even breathe too deeply.

"Who the fuck puts people in a crazy cage and sets traps?!" The girl next to me yells/whispers. My body shakes at the thought of just what kind of person *would* do that.

"A sick fuck." I reply so only she can hear the answer to her rhetorical question.

All the girls back up slowly, heading further into the room, not wanting to risk their lives with the unknown. I lean against the wall, my muscles tight and my palms sweating. How are we going to get out of here? A moment of helplessness works its way through me, and I want to give into it and just sit down. I can feel the tears stinging the back of my eyes.

We sit in silence for what has to be a few hours, all of us lost in our thoughts and misery. It's hard to know for sure without any windows to see any light to judge the time by but it sure feels like hours. A few girls mumble things to themselves while others cry silently. I however do none of those things. My spine straightens as I rack my brain for a way out of this. *There has to be a way out of this.* As if answering my unspoken question, a TV I hadn't noticed that was disguised as a painting comes to life. A masked person comes into view and once it speaks you can tell it's using voice distortion because his voice sounds animatronic.

"Hello Ladies," it starts as if this is an everyday fucking event, and for him, it just might be. "As you can see, by your friend over there." It waves vaguely in the direction of our dead fearless leader before continuing. "There are traps placed throughout the Maze, it is your job to figure out the puzzles to make it through safely." He pauses long enough for us to absorb what it is that's being said. "If you can solve all the puzzles and make it out of my Maze alive... then you can have your freedom. If not... Well, it will cost you your life." It's hard to tell with the blood-red purge mask he has on, but I sense he's smiling behind it. "Let's see if you're clever enough to outsmart me." An evil chuckle seems to continue even after the screen reverts back to a painting.

"No... No! N-no fucking way. I'm not doing this!" Someone shouts as if the masked figure will hear it. "Let me out!" she screams at the top of her lungs, and the sound seems to clang around the small room, causing my head to pound. "I won't do this!" she keeps yelling nonsense and I have a weird feeling that whoever it is can hear her but won't dignify her with an answer.

It's play the game and chance dying, or stay here and die anyway. Either way, we're fucked.

"Okay, so it said it's a puzzle. Is anyone good at puzzles?" I ask, trying to see if we can make progress because the idea of not trying and dying slowly of starvation is something I'm not willing to do. Not yet at least. The girls look around as if I just asked a classroom of kids a question and no one wants to raise their hand to answer it.

Finally, a soft voice that I don't think has spoken yet says, "Me." Her voice is so soft I can barely make it out, if I hadn't seen her slightly raised hand I wouldn't even have known it was her that spoke.

"Okay, excellent. That's a start." I try to force a smile of encouragement, having somehow become the co-captain.

"What kind of puzzle do you think it is?" Another girl asks.

I scrutinize the room some more, paying close attention to all the objects. It looks like some grandma's storage locker, with antique bookcases and ugly nicknacks.

It's then I notice some strange markings on the wall that I wrote off as graffiti originally. I make my way over to one and see that it appears to be some type of symbol. It makes no sense to me.

"Anyone have any clue what this symbol could mean?" I ask the room, my eyes still fixated on the wall.

The quiet girl who said she was good at puzzles steps up and stands beside me, her eyes flashing back and forth to the other symbols around the room like she's doing a particularly difficult mathematical equation. I try to follow her eyes as if I too can figure out what's going through her head just by mimicking her. Nope. Still nothing.

Her eyes brighten and a look almost like excitement passes across her face. "I think I got it!" she mumbles softly and then she's searching the room again, moving things around.

"What are you looking for? I thought you figured out the puzzle?" I ask, baffled as to what the fuck is going on. She just shakes her head and continues to mumble softly under her breath. The girl's got a few screws loose.

"Ahh Haa!" She raises her hand, but I don't see anything. It's not until she starts writing on the wall I see it was a piece of chalk that she must have just found. She's combining all the small symbols to make one large one.

"Oh. Shit..." I grumble as I start to catch up. She makes a few different combinations before she seems to settle on one.

"I think that's it." She whispers but her face seems less excited and more fearful than before.

"Okay? So what's it mean?" I finally speak after a few minutes of awkward silence where there should be an explanation.

She slowly turns around so she's facing the others. "It's Greek." She finally states as if that explains it. When we continue to stare at her dumbfounded she continues. "It says, you won't win. In the Greek alphabet." Her head drops and I can tell she's freaked out by the message. A glance around the room tells me she's not the only one affected.

"Well, he's wrong. We will win and we *will* get out of here." I say in a voice firmer than I thought I could muster. Forcing confidence in my voice that I'm not entirely sure I feel.

The girls look skeptical but are willing to hang on to some hope... at least for now.

"Anyway, how does that help us get out of here?" A tall blonde says. "Hey! Asshole...How does that help us get out of here? We solved your stupid fuckin' puzzle now let us out!" She shouts her head angled towards the ceiling. We all wait in silence to see if the masked madman responds, but of course, it remains silent.

"I don't get it. I solved it correctly, I'm sure of it." The quiet one is muttering to herself once again.

"Are you sure you got all the symbols?" I look around again, a few of the girls start moving pictures and we end up finding more of the Greek symbols. After about ten more minutes of translating we have, "Duck, then add eight." the mumbler rubs at her forehead as equally confused as the rest of us.

"Add eight what? What the fuck does that even mean?" A few of the girls are openly angry, while others are still sobbing.

"Well, these are Greek symbols and if I'm not mistaken they are considered mathematical symbols, right?" I say hesitantly, I'm pretty sure I read that somewhere, hoping I don't sound like an idiot.

"Some, but not all." A beautiful sandy blonde replies as she steps forward toward me.

"Well, does duck mean something in math?" I scratch my head, now I know I sound stupid.

The shy girl who translated it all snorts out a laugh before quickly covering it with her hand. "Not that I know of." She finally says after she gets herself together and stops laughing at me.

"Are there any ducks in this room?" I ask the only other thing I can think of that the masked psycho might mean. "I feel like he's being intentionally obtuse to confuse us." I huff.

"Oh that, I definitely agree." The shy girl points to the wall of chalk-drawn symbols. "Some of these are capital while others are lowercase. At first, I thought it meant that they were the start of a new word, but no. He did it because he chose letters that wouldn't look obviously like letters." Her hand traces over one letter in particular. "See, N in capital looks like an N but in lower case, it looks more like a V. He did that intentionally to throw me off, or well, us off." She corrects.

"Well, there is a wire there, do you think it means duck literally? As in under the wire?" another girl pipes up and it's like a light bulb goes off in all of our heads. Well, duh. Jesus, he's already fucking with our heads. I bet that's exactly what he wants. I say him because honestly, the width of his shoulders and the way the voice distortion couldn't quite hide the depth of his deep voice leads me to believe it's a male.

"So, we just duck under the wire and take eight steps?" A girl says as she is already walking towards the opening.

"Possibly, but it's what comes after those eight steps that has me worried." I suppress a shiver. As much as I'm trying to put on a brave face for the rest of the girls, it's fucking hard to be a leader. It's hard to hold the hope of all eleven girls on my shoulders when I have no more of a clue than they do about why the fuck we are here or what's going on.

A few of the girls follow the other girl towards the exit, while others stay rooted to the cement floor beneath them.

"Better the devil you know than the one you don't." One girl says as she plops herself down on the floor and a few others nod with her before joining her. As much as I'm inclined to agree with her, I also want to get the fuck outta here.

"I think we just need to keep our eyes peeled and watch every little step we take. He's already made it clear he's a lunatic and is intentionally fucking with us." I point out even though I'm not sure it even needed to be said.

I stare at the opening for a few long moments before I nod my head. "Let's do this."

Chapter Three

Nox

I watch on as most of the girls brave the Maze, a smile forming on my mouth. It's like watching rats. All you have to do is dangle the cheese–or in this case, freedom–and watch as they scurry to get it. With the thought of freedom on the line, they are willing to go against their instincts and self-preservation to achieve it. It really is quite fascinating if you're into that sort of shit. Me? I just like to play with my food before I eat it, metaphorically that is. I've never been big on cannibalism... I chuckle softly to myself at the image that provokes.

The maze is quite large and holds many turns and dead ends, ensuring its victims get lost and disoriented. After all, freedom is the prize but that doesn't mean it's achievable. I can feel the evil grin that rises to my face, knowing no one will survive the maze.

I don't even try to suppress my laugh as the girls gag and moan as they step over the body of their once brave leader. One girl even throws up, causing a few of the others behind her to cover their mouths, trying to keep whatever little they ate before being kidnapped in their stomachs. A wise choice since they won't be eating again.

I lean back in my office chair, taking deep breaths, as I watch the girls count each step to ensure they don't step into another one of my traps. The first puzzle is always the easiest. I do this for two reasons, one being, it gives them a false sense of confidence which tends to make them fight harder to escape, and two because well if they can't get out of the room, where's the fun in that?

The girl who was yelling loudly that she wouldn't do my Maze takes a sudden step to the left to make room for the other girls and accidentally steps right into the bear trap that closes rapidly on her thin ankle. I can hear the metal teeth of the contraption snap as they come together around her leg. Her tortured screams are loud and play like music in my ears. I can feel my pulse speed up as I can almost smell the blood that pours from her now open wound. My cock thickens in my pants and I give it a gentle squeeze as if reminding it there is still so much more of the show to enjoy.

The new leader squeezes through the crowd of girls now surrounding the wounded one. The dark hallway is only lit by the fluorescent lights of the room they were just in, making it nearly impossible for them to see further into the maze or anything else around them.

"Be careful, only move backward not forward, we don't want to accidentally set off any more traps." She speaks as calmly as she can but her voice still quivers. I wish I could smell the fear, press my nose right up against it, and inhale until my lungs explode. I groan as I imagine how good it would smell. Mixed with the coppery scent of blood and perfume. I will admit the new leader seems to have a backbone, at least for now. That will change the further she gets into my Maze. The bravado can only last so long. Her hope will dwindle as more and more of her fellow females lose their lives.

She bends down to assess the damage the best she can in the low light. Her hands feeling around.

Thanks to the night vision on my cameras I can see with perfect clarity how the teeth have torn her soft flesh. The new leader feels around for a few more moments before she seems to find what she's looking for, she slips her fingers between the teeth and tries to pry it open.

"Fuck!" she grunts, as she pulls with all her might. "Someone help me!" she yells frustrated. When still no one moves she yells again, "What if it was you? Should we just let her bleed out because none of you have a fucking spine!?" Her anger's palpable. Finally, someone moves and reaches down for the other side and they work together to wedge the two sides apart.

There's a squeak of the hinges before the sides finally pull away from the girl's leg. The two girls pant at the exertion used to open it. The one who was trapped yelps as it pulls away and the blood gushes harder now that the teeth aren't there to keep the wound somewhat sealed.

"We've got to stop the bleeding." A new girl speaks up. "Anyone have a belt?" The girls shift slightly as they pat down their waists.

"Yes!" Another one shouts as she pulls it from her pants. The new girl immediately takes it and starts wrapping it tightly about the wound.

"Are you sure you should be doing that?" A faceless voice from the crowd asks.

"Yes. I'm a nurse. What I'm doing is creating a tourniquet to reduce the blood flow to her lower leg. Hopefully, the wound will clot and the bleeding will eventually stop." she explains.

"Good. That's smart." The new leader says as she nods her head once. "We've got to keep moving." She looks around at the walls, well, what she can see of them. "You think there's another puzzle around here?" She asks as if the others can see better.

"That or he wants us to think there is." The forever pessimist pushes through her clenched teeth as the nurse continues to crank the tourniquet as tight as it will go. "Fuck! That hurts." she cries out.

The leader shushes her and tries to comfort her by holding her hand. I roll my eyes. That comradery will diminish, and soon they will be throwing each other into traps to try and gain their freedom. Anything to survive. I've seen it in the past and I relish the moment it happens again. They slowly continue down the hallway until they reach the first right turn. They follow behind each other like little ducklings following their mother. I roll my eyes at the pathetic sight.

They take the next right, and getting rather bored, I open a file on my computer called Extras and start inserting the code to tell the program which area I want one of my surprises to go off. Once I get that all put in, I wait until the girls are all standing relatively near my new party favor. My finger hovers over the Enter button, my pulse throbs and my palms sweat with excitement. My cock stiffens in my pants and the anticipation of hearing their screams of possible bloodshed makes me groan out loud.

"Gotcha," I whisper as my finger slams down on the button. There is dead silence for the space of a heartbeat before the loud roar of chainsaw buzzing floods the air. The girls shriek. I close my eyes so I can take in each girl's scream. Even though they are all at once, the tones are different and I take pleasure in hearing each and every variation. The song of their wailing comes together like Beethoven's 5th Symphony. My eyes roll back behind my lids as my hands naturally lift as if I'm conducting the sounds myself. And in a way, I suppose, I am.

This is where I should say it feeds my inner beast, but I don't have an inner *anything.* My insides are empty. A black void that feasts on the suffering of others and nothing more. It will never be fulfilled or satisfied. Like a black hole, a combusting star that causes everything around it to combust with it, leaving behind only darkness and destruction. It's always been like this, no matter how much my parents tried to dissuade me from my perverse obsession with all things dead and dying. Nothing ever worked. Eventually, they just resorted to covering it up. I guess having a shit ton of money has its advantages.

I open my eyes to watch as the girls try desperately to avoid the teeth of the saw, trying to back up without running into one another. There's one blade on each side of the narrow hallway, they glide back and forth along the wall for about four feet, they overlap and there's a foot gap between each of the saws' tips and the wall. The girls, not being able to see all this in the near pitch black have no clue if the blades will be able to reach them.

"Duck!" one of the girls shouts and they all drop to the floor. It's quite smart but the one closest to the blades accidentally gets pushed while the girl behind her throws herself down. She loses her balance and falls right into them, the spinning teeth rip at her flesh and tear through her like a chef's knife through a medium-rare steak. Her shoulder and chest split apart as her body jerks against the sharp rotating blade. Almost immediately her screams are cut off as she starts to gurgle on her blood. I watch entrapped as it pours past her lips and dribbles down her chin and quickly painting her shirt a deep red. The sight causes my cock to twitch against my thigh.

The new leader fumbles for the back of the girls' shirt but it's too late. The teeth have torn through to her heart. She falls to the ground with a heavy thud and there's a large pool of blood where her feet once stood. This means when the girls move forward they will need to crawl over her and through the blood to get past the saws. I'm delighted at how traumatizing that will be for them.

Deciding to show them a slight mercy, I turn on the low flood lights. They are sixteen feet apart and provide only a few feets worth of light before plunging them into total darkness once again. This is almost a hindrance to the girls at this point as their eyes had adjusted to the near darkness. They blink and try to will their eyes to work faster.

Soon they can see the chainsaws to avoid them. Which is a downside but I don't want this to end too soon. So, I will allow them this *one* advantage.

"We gotta get the fuck out of here." Another one of the girls shouts at the top of her lungs to be heard over the roaring of the chainsaws. The smell of gasoline permeates the air, causing some of the girls to cough and sputter.

They scramble awkwardly to avoid the saws, but also the dead body, as they crawl under the rapidly spinning blades. For some of the girls, it's a close call, as they all rush and push to get past and away from the current danger. I watch on, stroking my cock as the girls wade closer to danger, the idea that more of them are going to die excites me in a way that only death can.

I grip my thick cock firmly in my palm, languidly stroking from root to tip, squeezing tighter as I go.

"Fuck," I grunt at the pleasure of having the blood forced into my dick. My eyes never leave the screen.

The one who seems to be in charge goes last, wanting to make sure everyone has gotten through safely. Just as she's directly under the blades, her ass lifts just enough to not only give me an amazing view up her short dress at the tiny strip of fabric barely covering her pussy, but it also causes the teeth to sink into her flesh. Her scream of agony as it does, causes my balls to tighten up and tingles to race down my spine.

"Oh, fuck." I grunt as I barrel toward an unexpected orgasm. The way her screams sound causes my fist to pump faster and I can't hold back any longer. My thick length pulses and jerks, I can feel it swell under my palm as cum sprays from the tip of my cock, coating the screen and her now panic ridden face that I have focused the camera on. My eyelids lower as I watch my jizz drip down the screen, coating her with my warm sticky essence and I can't help but feel like this is an omen. A vision of what's to come. I chuckle, no pun intended.

Using a rag, I wipe the screen but don't bother putting my wet cock away, I have a feeling I'm still going to need it.

She finally drags herself out from under the trap and stands. The light shows the blood that leaks from the wound. Coating the back of her dress and starting to drip down the back of her thighs. I groan. The sight of her thick juicy thighs covered in blood threatens to make my cock hard again.

"Fuck, are you okay?" One of the girls spins the leader around, checking her over, must be the nurse.

"I'll be fine." she forces through her teeth. The cut isn't super deep but I bet it hurts like a bitch. Knowing she will be suffering as she continues through my Maze makes a smile climb to my face.

The lights that I've turned on allow them to see they now have a decision to make. Left or right? I watch closely as they all turn towards their new leader, hoping she somehow has the answers to the unknown. I lean forward, intrigued. What decision will she make?

Her lip wobbles with indecision as her eyes flick from left to right, her mind trying to choose the best course of action.

"Should we split up?" she asks, nervously. Hoping someone else will make the decision for her. Relieving some of the pressure they have unknowingly applied to her shoulders.

"I don't know if that's such a good idea." The one that's being dragged along by two other girls says.

"Okay, so we move as a group." she nods her head as if it's decided. A few of the other girls nod along. Eager to keep moving.

"Let's go right." she shuffles forwards, emboldening the other girls to do the same. The hallway goes on for a while with nothing, tricking the girls into a false sense of comfort.

"Maybe this is a dead end..." someone speaks up.

"Yeah... It seems too quiet. Something's up." another one agrees.

It's then that a two-foot by two-foot scale embedded in the floor comes into view. Slightly raised but doesn't look obviously like a scale, that scale is attached to an iron gate that has extremely sharp spears on the bottom. They need to figure out how to distribute the weight properly on the scale to lift the gate, but sacrifices will have to be made to get underneath it safely.

I watch as the women slowly creep forward, testing the object on the floor.

"What the fuck is that?"

"Probably some kind of booby trap."

"Careful not to touch it, just in case."

"How can we avoid it, it takes up most of the fuckin' pathway!"

The girls bicker back and forth, trying to figure out the best way to approach this new test. A cruel slant comes to my mouth as I sit back and enjoy the show. Just itching for them to turn on each other and the bloodbath to begin.

Chapter Four

Lenah

This shit is getting really old real quick. My fucking back hurts like a bitch and my dress is torn and I'm pretty sure my ass is hanging out. Not that it matters when you're fighting for your life, but it certainly adds to the level of aggravation coursing through my body like a shot of heroin. I'm starting to regret my decision to go out last night. If I had just stayed in and told Jenna to go fuck herself–like I wanted to–when she begged me to go out with her, I'd be sitting at home with a good smut book and probably be at least one orgasm down by now. But, nooo... instead I'm here in a literal hell.

I shake off those thoughts, they aren't going to change the situation and they certainly aren't helping me get out of here. I roll my shoulders back, trying my hardest to ignore the pain in my back as I push on.

"There's a gate, we're trapped."

"Try and lift it."

"Fuck, it's so heavy, I don't think I can. Someone help me." multiple girls are grunting and groaning as they struggle to lift it. "It's too heavy." Five girls are lifting now and still no luck. My eyes glance at the raised pad on the floor.

"Does anyone have anything we can put on it? Figure out if it will cave in or trigger something?" I ask the rest of the girls, my eyes flashing around trying to take in all of their freaked out faces. The faces of the girls I may or may not make it out of this alive with. I try to study their faces just in case I have to describe them to the police. That is... if I get out of here.

The girls are patting down their clothes, but everyone comes up empty. "We could use a shoe but I don't want to risk going barefoot in this death trap," I grunt, speaking to myself out loud. "Okay...Okay." I have an idea. I grab the strongest looking girl, "Hold my arms tight, whatever you do, Don't. Let. Go!" I stare her down making sure she understands just how fucking serious I am. She nods once.

Holding onto her arms, I slowly move my foot over the square bump-out on the floor. I press down on it lightly, quickly pulling my foot back as fast as I can in case something falls, or the ground gives way. I wait a few seconds, and when nothing happens I try again, applying a little more pressure before pulling back once more. It's after the third time and more weight that I hear it, the faint sound of metal hitting stone.

"The gate! It lifted!" one of the girls shouts, excitement clear in her voice.

"It's a scale!" another one yells.

Still not willing to trust my full weight on it. I dare to put a good chunk of my weight on it this time, holding it for a moment longer. When nothing happens but we hear the slight clang again, I finally chance it, and stand directly on it, causing it to lift slightly higher. "We need more weight." I realize. But then a horrible thought occurs to me. Not all of us are going to make it to the other side if we have to keep the weight on the scale. My eyes slam closed and I swallow hard. I'm not sure the other girls have figured this out yet and I don't want to freak them out by wearing my fear on my face.

Two more girls get on the scale with me and the gate lifts about two feet off the ground.

"Hurry go! Go!" I shout, encouraging them to crawl under the gate. The girls emboldened by my words scurry under but stick close to it just in case something is waiting on the other side.

Smart choice.

Once all the girls are through but the three of us left on the scale. I say, "Okay, you two run!" I all but shove them off.

"No! We need to figure out a way for all of us to get through." one of the girls argues while the other needs no more encouragement and is already halfway under the gate, that's now only about a foot and a half off the ground.

"Can you guys try to hold it now that it's already up?" I ask, practically begging for a way for all of us to make it through this. A few of the girls step up trying to hold it up but the second we go to step off of it drops dramatically, leaving the gate only a few inches off the ground.

"Fuck!" the girl beside me hisses as we both step back on the scale. "You go, they need you more than me," she says only loud enough for me to hear. My eyes widen at her selflessness.

"That's not true. There has to be a way for us all to get out of here, we just have to play this smart." I know I'm clutching at straws but I'm not willing to give up hope, not yet.

"Lift higher," I beg the girls, as more girls step up they can lift it. "Run!" I shout to the girl next to me, we both dive to the floor, the gate only a few feet from where we stood, "Come on, hurry!" I'm almost completely under when I hear screaming and the gate drops slightly, I yank my leg past the gate just in time for it to come crashing down.

A blood curdling scream rips past the lips of the girl who was just behind me. My eyes flicker to the gate, which is now lodged in the girl's pelvis, pinning her to the floor as blood rapidly pools around her.

She's choking as screams force their way past her lips. "I-it h-hurts." she cries as blood paints her lips and teeth red.

"Come on, help me. Lift, lift!" I scream. I reach down, cutting my hands on the sharp blades that are protruding from the bottom. As many girls as we can fit, squeeze in and help me lift. It lifts but only a few inches. It's so fucking heavy, my face turns red from exertion as I put all my effort into it, but it's still not enough.

"I can't hold it much longer." another girl grunts and a few whimper in agreement.

"Fuck!'' No matter what we do it's not enough. It slips from my grip, slicing my palms as everyone lets go simultaneously, causing it to slam back down into the poor girl's back. She remains silent as her body twitches, the blood now spreads out the full width of the small corridor and I'm positive she must be gone.

"We're not all going to make it out of this are we?" The quiet girl who figured out the first puzzle whispers. My heart crumbles, knowing she's right. Everyone remains silent, no one wanting to admit that gruesome fact. Not wanting to acknowledge the odds of our fate.

"Let's keep moving. The longer we stand around the longer we are trapped in here." My eyes scan the walls, knowing there's bound to be another trap around here somewhere. When I don't see anything I proceed with caution. After about twenty steps I see there is another right and a left. The right has one flood light that seems to be darker than the others, barely illuminating anything and the left is completely dark. *Fuck.*

We slowly move forward, our little group clinging together like a group of nats in the summer. There are only ten of us left, and we are still supporting the girl who was caught in the bear trap. It's getting harder and harder to carry her dead weight though and every time I look back her eyes seem to droop even more, putting more and more weight on the two girls beside her.

The girl on the right catches me staring, "I don't know how much longer she's gonna last," her voice sounds sad as she readjusts the girl hanging limply with her arm draped over her shoulder. The girl on the left grunts slightly as she momentarily has to hold more of the weight. I stop, causing the other girls to do the same, unsure of which direction to go.

"She's slowing us down," the girl to the left says sternly. And even though it's true I don't like the tone she uses as she admits this. "I'm sorry but I can't risk my life for a girl who's going to die anyway." she huffs, ducking and freeing herself from the wounded girl's weight.

"Fuck," moans the girl on the right who is now hunched over with the burden of all the weight. "I...can't do... it... alone," she pants the weight getting to her. When no one steps forward to help, I do. Taking over for the other girl, splitting her weight between us. My back screams in protest from where the blood has started drying over the wound. The pain is so immense, I grind my teeth together to keep from crying out.

"Keep m-moving." I finally grind out as I force the pain back.

"Which way?" The girl now in front asks, looking back and forth.

"I don't fuckin' know. Pick one." I grunt, the pain and pressure getting to me and making me lose my patience.

The girls creep forward, taking another right and I feel the moment the girl between us takes her last breath, there's a deep stuttering inhale like she tried to take multiple breaths at once and her body goes completely limp. The air leaking out like a slowly deflating balloon. The other girl and I drop under the unexpected weight. "Fuck. Shit!" the other girl cusses as her knee hits the ground with a sickening crunch. I try to take more of the weight but my back isn't having it, I can feel the blood leaking down my legs. I have to let go. The body hits the floor with a loud thud and I cringe. Using my hands and my torn excuse of a dress, I apply pressure the best I can to the wound, trying to stem the flow of blood.

"We have to keep moving. The longer we stay here the more of us will die." the girl limps beside me, and I'm pretty sure she broke her knee. Her pained eyes meeting mine. As much as it sucks I know she's right. Quite a few of us need medical attention, plus in a place like this, you're just asking for an infection. I take a deep breath, my head dropping back on my shoulders as I stare at the endless darkness above me. I have no clue how far the walls are or where this death trap of a maze is located, everything is pitch black, outside of the small bursts of light the flood lights admit. I close my eyes and for the first time in my adult life, I say a prayer. The long sordid history with God notwithstanding.

Flashes of my father locking me in my room with a bible and nothing else, flicker through my mind. My mother on Sunday morning in a powder blue cape dress and bonnet. She always wore blue on Sundays. Her long blonde hair twisted up in a tight bun beneath the bonnet. Her eyes were downcast as she urged me forward, my identical powder blue dress hitting my tiny ankles as I hurried to keep up with Father. The small woven satchel I always carried, hitting my hip with my rapid movements. "Schiet op, kind," he tells me to hurry up in Dutch as I straggle behind. My short legs, not able to keep up.

"Come on, move." the girl beside me nudges me forward and we start moving again.

"Keep your eyes open for traps," I say needlessly, it's not like we aren't all on high alert.

Once we reach the dull light, a sinking feeling forms in my gut. Something isn't right. The moment that thought pops into my head, I hear a grinding noise and the walls start to close on either side of us.

"Fuck. RUN!" I scream as I push and shove the girls back in the direction we came.

A few of the girls run forward, hoping to outrace the walls. I don't bother to stop and change their minds. I hear the deafening sound of crunching and screaming as I reach the hallways we just left. I lean forwards onto my knees, my heart racing and my breath escaping me in rough pants. We all seem to collectively continue on. Not wanting to acknowledge the awful sounds we all just heard.

After only a few more steps I hear a weird whooshing sound. "What is that?" I whisper to the now smaller group of girls around me.

"I don't know. It kind of sounds like something cutting through the wind." Her head cocks to the side and she listens further, trying to place the unknown sound.

"Stop!" I yell, as the sound gets louder the closer we get.

"I think I know what it is." One of the girls near the front whispers as she gulps audibly. "Anyone ever read Edgar Allen Poe?" And suddenly that sound makes sense. The pendulum blade that hung over the man in one of his stories.

"Fuck." I cuss as I picture a blade swinging in utter darkness before us. How the fuck are we going to avoid something we can't see? It's as the girls come to a complete stop and silence permeates the air that I hear it. Very subtle but it's there. *Tick-Tock, Tick-Tock*. This motherfucker took the pit and the pendulum is a DIY guide. "It's a clock. Listen to the ticks." I murmur, pitching my voice low so they can hear it.

"So, do we move between the ticks? That's only like half a second!" The panic reverberates through the girls like a wave crashing on the shore.

"How are we going to do this?!" Whispers and half-baked ideas trickle to me in the back as everyone tries to come up with a way out of this. All we have to go on is the ticks and the whooshing sound as it swings back and forth. Other than that we are blind. We all stand there listening to the ticks as if that will somehow give us the answer.

"I need out. Get me the fuck out!" A girl who was relatively silent the whole time shrieks as she lurches forward, her arms shoving the other girls aside. The few girls closest to the front let out blood-curdling screams and in the blink of an eye she's in front of us and she must have triggered a sensory light because we can see her in all her glory. Her body frozen in time as if hit with some sort of freeze ray. We all collectively hold our breath as gravity finally kicks in again and her body drops to the floor in two separate increments.

"Oh god," one girl mumbles and it sounds like she's about to throw up. Not that I blame her. We just witnessed a body being cut in half. Her brain, visible from where it lay on the cold concrete floor. The slice is so precise that it isn't until a few seconds later that blood starts to begin pouring from her body. Multiple girls end up vomiting and I'm fighting back my own as my eyes slammed shut. The pendulum keeps swinging as if nothing happened, just cutting more and more pieces out of the body lying beneath it, spraying blood up onto the walls. I duck my head as my eyes remain closed, not able to look at it any longer.

Tears flood some of the girls' eyes as they mourn the loss of one more of us, at least with the others we hadn't had to watch it happen. The helpless, trapped feeling truly sinking in. We stand there, sobbing and whimpering as we listen to the ticking of the clock.

Ding-dong, ding-dong…Ding-dong, ding-dong. Dong, dong, dong, dong, dong, dong. The chime echoes through the space, giving us a brief idea of the size of the area we are trapped in. Which is quite large if the echo is anything to go by.

"Six." a girl whimpers next to me.

"What?!" my eyes flash to what I can make of her face in the low light.

"Oh… Ugh… It's six o'clock." She looks around at everyone staring at her in absolute shock. "My grand-mother used to own a grandfather clock. It chimed just like that." She looks away, shy under our scrutiny.

"Tell us everything you know about the mechanics of grandfather clocks," I say as I shake her almost violently as if I can shake the answer loose and find us a way out of here.

"I'm sorry... I d-don't know much. I just know it dinged on the hour and every fifteen minutes to signal quarter after, half past, and quarter till. It also needed to be wound up to keep the time accurate." she murmurs her sad eyes carrying so much guilt that I drop my hands back to my sides.

"It's fine." I wave her off, it was a long shot anyway, I mean who studies clocks in their free time? My eyes wander the space as I try to think of a way out of this. It's then I notice the ticking has changed slightly, instead of *tick-tock, tick-tock*, It's *ticktock, ticktock*. "Wait...What did you say about it needing to be wound up?" My eyes flick back to her.

"Well, there were these weights on the back, three of them." she pauses for a second closing her eyes like she's trying to picture it in her head. "They would go all the way down and grandma would have to pull the slack to bring them back up when the rhythm would go off or the clock would..." Her eyes widen rapidly as she seems to put something together. "The clock would stop!" her hands shoot out to grip my biceps. "We can wait it out. I'm not sure how long it would take but if it's on a similar mechanism then it would eventually stop all on its own." She claps almost giddy at the thought of us being able to just wait this out. I have to admit I am too. The thought of losing more girls or even injuring more of us has my gut clenching. I can't help but take responsibility. I'm not entirely sure when I decided it was my duty to keep all these girls alive but I take the job seriously nonetheless and I plan to do just that.

"Okay. So we wait this out." I nod to the girls as I sink to the floor, making sure to stay clear of the blood that's riddled the floor. The others follow suit. I have to admit, the thought that we thwarted whoever the fuck is manipulating the literal slice of hell on earth brings a smile to my face. A few minutes into however long we will be waiting. Static crackles over what sounds like some sort of intercom, and a menacing laugh cackles. Causing chills up and down my spine and all my hairs to stand on end. That's not the laugh of someone who is even remotely sane. No, that's, I just took a dive off the deep end and I'm bringing you with me kind of laugh. There are whimpers and whispers between the girls as we all subconsciously huddle closer together, seeking each other's warmth as his laugh chills us to the bone.

"Guy's certifiable," the girl beside me whispers. "Belongs in the looney bin." She turns to me and I nod my head in agreement. He belongs somewhere... whether it's prison or a mental institute the jury is still out.

"Lenah," I squeak out before clearing my throat and trying again. My awkward words breaking the lengthy silence. "My name's Lenah." I don't know why I feel the need to tell these strangers my name. Maybe it's because I may not make it out of here and I need someone to know who I am, someone to remember me. My family wouldn't even know I was dead... not since they completely disowned me. I clear my throat of those sad thoughts along with the lump that was lodged in it.

"Kate," another girl speaks up.

"Jennifer, but everyone calls me Jen," the nurse says.

"Megan."

"Ava."

"Amelia."

Once everyone introduced themselves a calm seemed to settle over the group. As if now we aren't just a group of strangers but friends, comrades.

After the clock dings two more hours, I notice the ticking is completely different now and the whooshing seems to slow down.

"I think it's working," Megan says as we all turn to the pendulum which is indeed slowing down. We've all somehow agreed that we wouldn't stare at it. I'm not sure if that was due to the horrific sight below it or if it's a watched pot that never boils type of situation or maybe even just not wanting to get our hopes up in case this is all a waste of time, but we all did it.

"We can probably move past it now. Just move quickly and carefully." I count how long it takes the jerky pendulum to reach the other side. It takes about five seconds. "Okay, Jess, you go first." I nudge her back softly to encourage her to go. She waits till it's on the left then shoots past on the right. "1...2...3...4...5." I count as the next girl goes.

I take a deep exhale as we all make it to the other side. The air smells of copper and death but I ignore that as I pull all the oxygen I can back into my lungs. *We made it.* We survived one more of his wicked traps. Eager to make up for the time spent waiting for the clock to slow, we pick up our pace and scurry along. The pitch black encasing us once again as the floodlights are so far apart.

My nerves are strung tight as I scan back and forth over the entirety of the space. My eyes strain as I scan rapidly, swinging back and forth, not wanting to miss a thing. I open my eyes as wide as I can, trying to force more light into them, begging for a scrap of detail to alert me of the unknown dangers. My hands shake as adrenaline surges through me. We've been walking for what seems like too long. Much too long to go without a trap based on the distance the other traps were set.

My pulse pounds and my heart races, causing my palms to sweat as I wait for something to spring out or for someone to suddenly drop dead.

"It's been too long," Jess I believe says under her breath, echoing my thoughts.

"I'm scared," Jen murmurs in response, not acknowledging Jess' statement.

"Me too," I whisper back, no sense in denying it. The way the sweat is dripping down my back and my stomach clenches is more than enough proof, without the feel of imminent death hovering over my shoulder.

We slowly work our way towards another flood light. This one blinking ominously. Flashes of the last night I saw my mother and father blink through my mind.

"Wees voorzichtig, Lieveheersbeestje" Father's warning to be careful sounds as I rush ahead, eager to get to where we are going. The flame of the torch lights flickering as we pass, making our way down to the village center. Our community may be small but we all work together to serve each other. Mr. and Mrs. Cline, work the butcher shop, while Ellis and Levi's parents, till the large fields just north of our tiny town. Everyone has a job that looks out for us all.

Tonight Father has off and we are going to get cream sodas from the little shop that sells homemade candies and sweet treats. Father and Mother only let me have them on special occasions and today is a very special occasion as it's my birthday! I skip, my shoes kicking up dirt as I try not to rush too far ahead.

"Vertragen, Lieveheersbeestje," Father chuckles softly as he tells me to slow down. He always calls me Ladybug when he's in a good mood. I breathe a sigh of relief that I haven't done anything to aggravate him in my excitement. Mother stays silent beside him, ever his subservient observer. I glance quickly at my shadow as it shifts size and shape slightly with the flickering of the flame from the lamp. Pausing a second to admire it before I continue skipping on. I only stop once I reach the front door of the sweets shop. The Open sign swaying softly on the door from whoever had just entered. I wait for Father and Mother to catch up before opening the door for them to enter, following dutifully behind them.

"Avond, Margaret," Father greets the shop owner with a slight dip of his head, the brim of his hat covering his eyes for a brief moment. I bound up to the counter, ready to place my order. Father grips my shoulder tightly before I turn my head to look at his disapproving face. I bow my head before stepping back, allowing him to order for us. I cower behind Mother as if she would protect me but I know she won't. I have irritated Father by forgetting my place. A woman's place is always behind a man, *his teachings reverberating through me. I will be punished for forgetting that lesson.*

A bang sound pierces the air causing Father to flinch, his order already forgotten as he shoves me and Mother behind him.

"Ga naar beneden!" he yells at us to get down. We follow as instructed. The bang sounds three more times before I hear screams and panic ensue. The door chimes as an unknown masked man enters the shop, aiming a large gun at us.

"Give me the money! Everything you got!" he shouts as he tosses what looks like a burlap sack into the counter in front of Mrs. Margaret. She shivers and shakes and I know Father is silently seething at the disrespect of this unknown man, but he makes no move to defend her. Not yet.

His eyes never leave the strange man, as Margeret slowly fills the sack with money from the register. The man's eyes slide to me before dropping down to my chest. At sixteen my breasts have finally started to grow large enough to need the support of a bra and although they are completely covered, I can't help but feel the burning heat of his stare as it seems to penetrate my cape dress. It's as if he's stripped me bare. I gulp and try to subtly cover myself, unsure how I feel about his leering. A slight growl escapes Father's lips, causing the masked man's eyes to swing to his. And although I can't see his masked face, I can still tell he's smirking beneath it. Once the bag is full, Margaret pushes the sack back towards him. He snatches it off the counter and Father seizes the opportunity to bound forward, slamming his shoulder against the outsider. Causing him to stumble slightly, his large muscular frame more solidly built than Father's. He easily gets the upper hand, planting the mouth of the gun against Father's chest before rapidly pulling the trigger. The sound so loud my ears ring and on instinct I crouch covering my head as my mouth opens. The sensation of knowing sound is leaving my mouth but not being able to hear it builds my fear even more.

It isn't until I'm yanked up by my arm that I finally start to hear my voice pierce the air. The pitch high and desperate, like the swallows that have perched near my bedroom window.

"Shut up!" he yells in my face as he yanks me over the bodies of my now deceased parents. My mother lay haphazardly over my Father as if even in death she's protecting him. My eyes widen as I take in the blood that pools beneath them, the soft soles of my shoes soaking up their blood like a sponge, causing me to slip and slide on the floor of the shop. I try to fight off the interloper, to no avail. He's too strong. His tattooed fingers gripping me too tightly.

"Let go! Please!" Words I've never dared speak to Father pass my lips as the large man drags me towards the door. I pull and slide, leaving long streaks of blood along the floor. My eyes turn to the counter, silently begging Margeret to help me, but all I see is her limp arm splayed across the floor *where it peeks out from behind the bottom of the counter. I'm alone.*

"You're not getting away," he chuckles, no remorse or pity in his voice as he yanks me from the only life I've ever known...

My brain filters back as the flickering light turns solid for a long moment before blinking again. The ground shudders below us and I know the other shoe has dropped. Within the space of three heartbeats, a stone wall is erected in front of us. Its solid block surface, leaving no footholds for us to even attempt to climb it.

Chapter Five

Lenah

"We have to work together. These tasks seem to be more about outsmarting him than just making it through. He's...testing us." I don't realize what I'm saying is true until the words pass my lips. Clicking a few of the puzzle pieces together while adding a few more to the pile of unknown.

"What the fuck is he testing us for?"

It's a reasonable enough question, but one I don't have the answer to. "I have no clue," I honestly answer.

"Let's just focus on completing this task and not so much on the why. There's no way of knowing what's going through a psychopath's mind." Megan reasons. I nod, knowing she's right.

"Okay, so, have any of you by any chance done cheerleading?" I look around the group and Ava perks up, a look of understanding crossing her face. She stands beside the wall, lacing her fingers together while crouching down, bracing herself to lift. The other girls, quickly catching on, make room as they each wait their turn. Jen is lifted into the air and we wait with bated breath to see what happens...

"Shit!" she hisses, "There's about two more feet to the top." I can see her stretching but the floodlights aren't hung high enough for us to see the top. Ava sets her back down and I step up beside her, taking her hands in mine and lacing them together.

"Ready to launch some girls." I give a soft smile, trying and failing to lighten the heavy mood that clings to all of us. She gives me a soft smile in return, humoring me. Jen steps back up and on the count of three, we bounce slightly before giving her a toss into the air. I can hear the moment her hands slap the top. She grunts as her feet push against the wall to try and help her arms pull her weight up. She struggles for a bit before finally she pants and announces her victory. We repeat this process. Jen waits at the top to help to pull the girls up before holding them as they lower their bodies to drop down the other side.

We all breathe a collective sigh of relief when we all reach the other side safely. It was tricky when it came to Ava and me. Jen ended up holding onto the far side and dangling her body over the edge while I held her feet. Ava crawled up our bodies like a ladder before I climbed up.

Pulling Jen's exhausted body up too.

We all pause for a moment to catch our breaths when a loud static sound echoes through the maze. A screen none of us had noticed embedded in the wall flickers to life. The purge masked man's face appears a moment later.

"Congratulations on making it this far." he appears to look around intimidatingly. I find my lip lifting in a snarl as I think about all the shit this fucker has been putting us through. All the lives that have been lost for his amusement.

"What the fuck do you want from us? Why are you testing us?" The questions escape my lips before I have a chance to hold them back. My anger takes the front seat as I watch him in disgust. I don't know if he can hear me but I hope to God he can.

He tilts his head, almost mockingly, as if looking down at a young child trying to explain something as simple as one plus one. That stupid smile of the mask covering his mouth, helping to distort his voice as he replies, "Because I can." He pauses for a moment as if enjoying the rage that sets my skin on edge. I can feel it bubbling through the other girls as well.

"Now, as I was saying. Congrats on your accomplishment. I must admit, I am minorly impressed by the amount of you left. But don't worry, that will change." His eyes flicker with amusement as he continues. "You have made it to the halfway point. But I feel I must warn you, it gets harder from here." he laughs, excitement causing him to sound almost giddy.

"You sick, Fuck!" I roar. My fists clenching so tight, half moons form on my palms where they dig into my flesh. Never in my life have I felt the desire to kill someone, but I can say with full conviction that if I make it to the end of this thing, I will look for him. And I will kill him. I find myself excited for the first time since I woke up in the maze. The hunger to feel his warm blood spilling from his neck, as my shoulders shifting back and my breaths quickening.

As if sensing my inner thoughts, his gaze focuses on me. "Oh, you haven't even begun to experience the lengths my sickness goes. I relish the thought of you feeling the pain my maze is going to inflict on you. You will earn your freedom with every drop of blood and shred of flesh. I will ensure it." without waiting for a response the screen flickers gray before going completely black and disappearing back into the darkness of the shadows surrounding us.

I seeth. If this were a cartoon, smoke would be billowing out of my ears. Wave after wave of pure unadulterated fury crashes and batters my insides, like a hurricane off the coast, causing destruction to anything and everything it touches.

"Come on, we gotta keep moving. You heard the psycho we are halfway there. That means there are six traps left." A new sense of determination courses through my veins.

Chapter Six

Basien (Bass-e-in)

T he door to the warehouse opens on squeaky hinges as I slowly push it in. Angry that Nox started the party without me. That fucker. My boots clomp on the concrete as I make my way over to the raised office space that Nox and I use to watch the girls.

I knock softly on the door, not wanting to interrupt him mid-tug. I know the sick fuck likes to jerk off to the girls as they fight for their lives. I grin as I open the door.

"I didn't say you could come in." he tosses back at me without even bothering to turn around.

"Well, good thing I didn't ask for your fucking permission then huh." I taunt back, knowing even with all his crazy he won't want to take me on. Although we both have what most people would consider psychopathic tendencies, my growing up in the streets taught me something that the prissy fucker could never gain while living in his mansions. Street smarts.

I can practically hear his eyes roll from here as I make my way closer. "What did I miss?" I bark knowing I missed a lot and I'm not fucking happy about it. He offers me a wry smile and I see him stroke his fat cock as he watches the screens.

"Oh, so much, brother." he taunts and If I didn't love him, I'd fuckin' kill him, honestly I still might. I pull a pack of smokes out of my back pocket, putting it in my mouth, and lighting it up before handing it to him. He takes it before giving me a nod in thanks. "They are halfway through." he finally says as he blows out a puff of smoke.

"Is she still alive?" I ask, my lungs pinched tight in my chest and it has nothing to do with the cig I just lit up.

He snorts out a sound of derision. "Of course she is." I blow out a breath as I study the girls on the screen. They are moving with more determination than I would've expected at this point in the maze. "I pissed her off." he chortles as he takes another deep drag. I throw my head back and laugh imagining her angry face. Of course, he did. The fucker can't help but poke. I shake my head, that won't bode well for him. Oh, well.

The sight of her has my cock stiffening and I can't help but undo the button and zipper to relieve some of the pressure. Nox's eyes roam over my large frame, all my tattoos and scars on display since I hadn't bothered to throw on anything under my zip-up. His eyes come to a stop at the huge bulge in my black underwear that's now peaking through my undone jeans. I watch as his hand speeds up slightly and he squeezes hard enough for a bead of cum to form on the tip. We may be twins but with all my tattoos and more muscular frame, it's easy to tell us apart.

I lick my lips before yanking his head back by his hair. He grunts as my lips connect with his. Fuck he tastes so good. Mint with a hint of copper like he was licking up blood. While my mouth is caught up in his, I feel the sting of a knife as it cuts s line through my flesh. I moan into his mouth before he yanks himself back to draw in a deep breath. His finger slides through the belt loop around my waist and pulls me closer so he can lick the cut he made on my lower abdomen, right above my dick.

"Looks like you need some relief brother." he taunts as he stands and yanks my cock free from the confines of my boxers, his already out.

"I do. Maybe you should get on your knees and suck big brother's cock." I wink, knowing that it will piss him off that I mentioned our two minute age difference. Instead of responding he smashes our shafts together before using his hand to jerk us both off at the same time while grinding them together. My head tilts back and I groan at the feel of his tight grip, of his soft velvety dick pressed against mine. "Goddamn that feels so good," I growl as I lean forward and bite hard onto his neck, making sure to draw blood from him just as he did me.

"Fuck!" he grunts before moaning.

"That's right. Always remember who's in charge." I snicker as I lap at the bloody mess I made of his neck.

"Fuck you!" he booms as he works our cocks faster. "I'm the one with your dick in my hand. I'd say that makes me in charge." he moves his body tighter against mine and I can feel his hardened nipples as they rub through his T-shirt to my bare chest.

"Ah…" rumbles through my chest before I can continue, "That's only cuz you can't get enough of my cock." I grunt as he squeezes harder, trying to hurt me but it only turns me on more. Not able to take it any longer I grab his hair and force him to his knees. I know he could fight me more than he is, but he wants my thickness in his mouth. So, even though he looks mad as hell he follows my unspoken command.

Once on his knees, he takes me into his mouth. With my hand still in his hair, I force myself as far as I can down his throat, holding his head still as I fuck his face. Not giving him any time to adjust as the base of my cock slaps against his lips over and over again. He gags and sputters and I feel his teeth gaze my dick in warning. My eyes nearly cross at the feel.

"So good at sucking cock. They teach you that in boarding school, little brother?" He bites again and I nearly blow my load. His hands grip my jean clad thighs as he eagerly works for my cum. I look down to see his eyes focused on me as his cock bobs freely between his legs in excitement. He goes to reach down to tug on it and I thrust my hips forward quickly, my teeth bared as I silently tell him not to touch himself. He snarls around my large shaft and it causes my balls to vibrate as he touches the base.

He's full-on humping the air, his lust so potent he can't resist. My eyes slide to the screen and I watch as she bends over, her short, slutty dress doing nothing to cover her plump round ass and It's all it takes for me to blow my load. I yank myself back just in time to spray Nox all over his face. I moan as It gets in his hair and drips off his chin. He opens his mouth wide, trying to get as much of my jizz as he can deep down his throat.

I smack his cheek with my now softening cock before shoving it back into his mouth to lick clean.

When he's done thoroughly licking me, he stands and grips his rigid length in his hand. "Now what the fuck am I going to do with this?" he grunts and I know he wants me to turn around and bend over. Too bad, I'm not the bitch in this relationship. I do reach forward, swiping as much of my cum off his face as I can before grabbing ahold of his cock and stroking him from root to tip.

His hips rock as his teeth clench. "Fuck, you do that so well. Learn that in prison big bro?" he mocks and I can't help the laugh that erupts from my lips.

"We both know I'm not the bitch." raising an eyebrow as I laugh at the cum smudged across his face and the bite wound still bleeding from his neck. He snaps, his anger rising and feeding his lust. His jeans sag farther down his thighs as he readjusts his stance, spreading his legs further apart for me. I lean in closer, my free hand going around his back to work my way between his cheeks. I run my finger over his clenched hole before pulling back and slicking that same finger, soaking it in my spit before returning. I force two fingers into his tight little hole, making sure to put pressure on his perineum.

"Fuck. Fuck!" he shouts as he blows his hot load all over my abs. His body jerking with the sheer force of it.

"You like my big tattooed, dirty hands on your dick and in your ass don't you?" I whisper in his ear, my voice deep.

"Fuck yeah," he says after he finally comes down. "It's like fucking myself but better." he chuckles and I can't help but laugh too. Not bothering to clean up the mess, I rub his cum into my stomach before putting myself away and plopping down in the chair he just exited. He, on the other hand, wipes his face clean. Probably not liking the stiff feeling of it drying on his face.

"She's beautiful isn't she," he says in awe as he stares at her through the monitor. I grunt in response. Her blonde hair is a tangled mess behind her and her eyes seem to shine even in the absence of light. I swear I can see her eyes twinkle with the struggle to hold back all the crazy. He pulls up another chair stuffing his limp dick back into his pants and sits down beside me. His eyes watch everything the girls do within the maze. No doubt obsessing about how he can improve it. I roll my eyes.

We've been doing this for years now. Kidnapping girls to put in the Maze. It's become a fun little game.

Not only finding and hunting the girls, but betting on who will live the longest, since none of them ever make it out. It's crazy how having money can make things disappear, just like magic.

Growing up it was never like that. Always bouncing from foster home to foster home, I never made it to a rich family. The only people that ended up with me are the people who needed the check from the state. That's all I ever was to them and that was fine. I didn't need anyone anyway. No one but Nox now.

"Being nostalgic brother?" he jokes as he shoves my chair, causing it to swing to the side slightly. I give him a side-eye. If you had asked me years ago if I believed in twin intuition or that twin telepathy bullshit I would have told you you were fucking nuts, but turns out we seem to have that shit cuz he always knows what I'm thinking.

"Maybe," I grunt, not wanting to admit I had slipped into my mind. He smirks, knowing I did.

We focus back on the monitors as the girls try to figure out the next puzzle. The floor is glass and lit from underneath. The piranhas that swim underneath the thin glass speed up as if sensing a meal is not too far away.

"What the fuck is that!" a girl screeches as she takes in the floor.

"Oh, chill out, it's just some stupid fish." A tall girl rolls her eyes before taking a cautious step forward, when nothing happens she puts more of her weight on the glass and takes a few steps forward the glass creeks under her weight but stays whole. She makes it to the other side and the next girl goes, causing the glass to crack softly.

"Fuck. Hurry up!" She shouts as she moves across the glass. the glass splitters further. She waits on the other side reaching out for the last girl. The second she steps onto the glass the whole thing shatters and she falls into the water. There's barely a splash before the slapping of fins is all you hear. Her body, bones, and all vanish before she has a chance to sink to the bottom.

The girls watch on in shock.

"I didn't know fish could do that!?" the little liar lies. I chuckle as my eyes swing to Nox's, he shakes his head but doesn't say a word.

The girls don't seem to mourn the loss for long, as they turn around and make their way further into the maze. As they reach the end of the hallway there is a right and a left. The right takes them back to almost the beginning while the left takes them one step closer to freedom.

"Five left." I smile. The excitement building inside me and if the stiffness in Nox's pants is anything to go by he's excited too.

"The best is yet to come." he's smug as he looks back at me both of us watching on.

Chapter Seven

Lenah

My rage, although slightly giving way to fear, continues to build in my chest. The need to get out of here with as many girls as possible burned through me. We have to make it. We have to.

"Left or right?" The remaining girls look to me to make the choice. I close my eyes tightly, knowing that if I'm wrong they'll need someone to blame for their pain but also need a leader to have the courage to make the decision. At this point, I'm so fucking confused. With all the twists and turns and dead ends, I don't even know how much farther we've gone.

"Left." My eyes flick open as I make the decision that could cost us all our lives. The weight bearing on my shoulders is enough to make me hunch forward.

"Shit." Jen hisses as a smack sounds out.

"What was that?" I ask, being in the dark we've become used to using our hands a lot more.

"Fucking wall." She grunts. "It's a 180 degree turn." She informs us, allowing us to avoid the same painful mistake she did. We barely turn the corner when a high-pitched hissing announces our next test. The whining is so loud it hurts my ears. There is a light barely touching the edge of something, it's sliding in and out of the light across the floor.

I carefully inch forward, now that there are only five of us left, there is more room to maneuver. It isn't until I'm right next to them that I see four circular saw blades jutting from the floor. There are staggers and they take up the whole hallway. They oscillate vertically along the floor leaving only a small gap between them.

"How the fuck are we supposed to get passed this!?" Meg shrieks.

"Can we walk between them?" Amelia, the one who figured out the first puzzle asks as she leans forward slightly to look.

"I can't tell. It's too dark." I huff.

"I swear to God if I get out of here I'm going to kill this guy." Jen growls and although no one says anything I think we all silently agree.

Amelia slides forward, her arms reaching across the width of the corridor, it's a little wider than her arms and I can't tell what she's doing until she kicks off her heels and lifts one leg pressing it to the wall before doing the same with the other. Once she seems to get her balance she works her way across, applying her weight to her legs to keep her elevated. She moves slowly and carefully until she reaches the other side. We all exhale at once and Jen goes next, mimicking Amelia's movements and brings her legs to the walls. When she's about halfway over Megan kicks off her shoes and goes.

The thought of being barefoot is not appealing to me, but I don't see any other option and I can almost bet this is not what the crazed lunatic had in mind when he built this death trap.

Megan moves a few feet before I hear the dreaded sound of something sliding against concrete. Jen yelps quickly in surprise as her left leg slips from the wall and she lands on her side directly onto a saw blade. Its rounded blade, quickly shredding her flesh and spraying blood and organs right up onto Megan who hoovers in shock above the now mangled body of Jen.

My body shakes and I gulp down the fear that that could be me. Meg doesn't move for a few moments and I notice her legs are starting to shake. "Hurry Meg, move." I encourage gently, not wanting to scare her or cause her to slip. The saws make a whining noise as they slowly eat into the remains of our fallen comrade.

It's dragging her body back and forth as it continues on its track. I close my eyes and swallow rapidly to keep the bile from coming up.

When Meg is almost to the light I take my turn. Trying my best not to look down and just focus on reaching the light. As I get closer I see Meg is about to misjudge the landing and hit the saw.

"Meg!" I shout but it's too late. Her foot lands on top of the blade and within seconds it cuts clean through the top of her foot. She screams as her body falls forward, no longer having balance without the front half of her foot. I scurry along until I make it well past where the blades end and even over Meg, just to be sure.

I crouch down, my hands going to Meg's wound as I try to apply pressure like Jen had taught us. Kate had followed close behind me and now was by my side trying to comfort Meg who is still screaming in pain. I try to speak calmly as I shush her, having a hard time focusing on what I'm doing with her yelling as loud as she is.

"I know it hurts. I know. I'm sorry. I'm trying." I beg as I apply more pressure to the wound that is quickly pouring from her foot.

Amelia stands back quietly and I can't help but wonder how she can be so calm. She has barely spoken this entire time. Her face seems oddly relaxed for being in such a horrific situation. I study her more closely. Watching as she stares on, at the mutilated bodies before her, like she finds them interesting.

Is it possible we've had the psycho with us the whole time? Wanting to watch the games up close and personal. Feel the blood splatter against her. I gulp. Will she try and kill us if we end up surviving this whole thing? Survive it, just to end up killed at the end of her knife. Oh, God.

As if sensing my eyes on her, her eyes meet mine, her head tilting as she gives me a soft smile. My eyes slide away from hers, unable to hold them. They wander down to her short dress, similar to mine. What was she doing before we were all kidnapped and placed in this maze?

"Everything okay, Lenah?" she asks but her voice almost implies that it's not a question but a statement. Saying without words to shut the fuck up. I nod my head dropping back down to focus on Meg's foot.

"We should just leave her. She won't be able to walk and we already know how this situation will end," she states calmly as if she's the voice of reason. I raise my head, meeting Kate's wide eyes.

"No, we can't just leave her!" she cries, her voice wobbly as she tries to regain her courage. Amelia's eyes meet mine again and the fear that races through me is stronger than I could have imagined. We've had a trader in our midst the whole time. I can see it now, so clearly. The question is why is she just revealing herself now? Is it because there are so few of us left that she has no one to hide behind anymore?

"We have to let her go..." I whisper as Meg's screams turn softer and softer. Kate's shocked eyes fly to mine.

"You're kidding me. You of all people. Our fearless leader!" her voice is laced with attitude and my head drops in shame.

"I never said I was fearless. I've been scared shitless this whole fucking time. But I also knew you all needed someone to stand up and take charge." I shrug gently, needing her to understand that I'm still me but I also need to try to get us out of this situation safely and that task just got ten times harder.

"Oh fuck you Lenah." she roars. Her hand lashing out seconds before connecting with my cheek. My head quickly whips to the side with the force but I don't make a sound. This...this is pain that I'm used to.

"She's already dying. But we...We are alive and I need to keep us that way." I widen my eyes slightly trying to get her to understand. Her eyes only narrow. With a large exhale I remove my hands from the now quiet Meg's foot and stand. Walking slowly past Amelia who has what appears to be a wicked grin on her face. Enjoying the turn of events.

"Hurry up, girls. Times a wasting." a voice echoes through the speakers, the inflection slightly different this time through the voice distortion.

Amelia chuckles this time and I can't hold back any longer. "Why!?" I all but yell as I whip around to face her.

"Why what?" her brows furrow and she fakes innocence.

"Why are you doing this?" I step closer. Willing to take my anger out on her if need be. If my suspicions are confirmed.

"I don't know what you're talking about Lenah." The way she said my name as if she's known me for years instead of hours. She leans closer, whispering in my ear. "We've been watching you," she smiles, letting her guard drop slightly. I pull back quickly, my eyes wide and directly on her. Her expression is blank again and she moves around me. Kate eyes me with blatant disgust and confusion. In an effort to get farther away from me, she moves ahead of Amelia.

"Oof," the sound escapes Kate's lips as she's suddenly yanked off her feet and now dangling from above us, her arms flailing around her. I instantly move forward reaching for her, but my fingers barely graze hers before she's yanked higher up and completely out of sight. Her screams get louder instead of softer as they echo through the open space above us. "Help!" she yells even though there is nothing we can do.

"Dropping like flies now," Amelia whispers to herself and I can't take it any longer. I draw my fist back and punch her dead in the face. She stumbles a few times before hitting the wall, a laugh bursting out of her.

"Does it just absolutely destroy you to know it was me all along." She pauses, smiling through the blood that's dripping out of her nose and into her mouth. "That I'm the reason you all are here." She tosses her head back and laughs harder.

"No!" I growl, even the thought causes my insides to ripple with anger.

Needed to get the fuck out of this maze I keep moving forward, carefully watching my steps because the traps seem to be getting closer now. Which I hope means I'm getting closer to the end. I keep moving forward, my focus on everything around me. It isn't until I feel the searing pain in my back that I realize I've been stabbed.

My knees give way as the pain courses through my back. "Fuck!" I yell, not knowing if I missed a trap or if that bitch just stabbed me in the back, literally and metaphorically. I fall to my knees but before turning around, my face connects with a knee.

Her deranged laugh is all I hear through the ringing in my ears and I'm right back to that night...

"You shut up and do what you're told and you might just make it out of this," he says and he forces my body into the trunk of his beat up car. "Such a pretty little thing. Would be such a waste," he murmurs to himself before slamming the trunk closed, encasing me in darkness.

I hear the door slam closed seconds before loud music starts to blast through the speakers, effectively drowning out any sounds I might make. I close my eyes and cry. Father may not have been the kindest man to me, and Mother never dared stood up against him but at least I knew what to expect. I have no clue where he's taking me or what will happen to me. I've never left our little village, not once, not even with Mother when she would occasionally leave to pick up odds and ends that we needed.

I'm not sure how long we drive before we are pulling over and he slams the car in park, causing my whole body to shift backward before smacking against the hard paneling. I can feel the blood oozing from the now cut on my forehead.

We must have been traveling for longer than I realized because when he opens the hatch again the bright light causes my eyes to burn. I scrunch my face and I blink rapidly, trying to relieve the sting from my eyes. Before they've even adjusted I'm yanked from the car. I'm pushed forward my upper half back into the trunk before he yanks my dress up and rips my white cotton panties down to my ankles. I swallow hard to keep down all the yells and protests I want to let free, knowing it will serve no purpose. This is what a woman is for after all. To serve a man, granted that man is usually your husband but to serve all the same. I've watched my mother and father a few times over the years, as she stayed dutifully quiet and never forgot her place.

"This sweet little pussy will be all mine. Almost better than the 1,500 I stole from that stupid little town of yours." he chuckles as he forces the blunt tip of what I'm assuming is his penis inside my tight opening. He grunts a few times as he tries to force himself in. "Damn, you're tight. You a virgin? Ain't no way I'm lucky enough to bag a virgin." he says in shock to himself. When I don't respond he smacks my ass hard. "Answer me, girl. You speak English?" he asks, having remembered that Father was speaking Dutch.

"Yes, sir," I murmur, not wanting to anger him further.

"Yes, what? Yes, you speak English or yes you're a virgin." He grunts as he forces more of himself inside me. I whimper before responding.

"Both." I force through gritted teeth. The pain almost too much.

"Ughhh..." he groans loudly as he slams his hips forward, pushing past my barrier and hitting the bottom of me. A *scream I was struggling to keep back forced its way past. "That's it, baby. You're mine now. You'll be my sweet little psycho."*

The nickname he gave me echoes in my ears as the pain draws me back to reality. Maybe it's time she finds out why he called me that, that day.

Dropping my mask I stand, reaching around to retrieve the knife that she left lodged in my back. I pull it free before my eyes connect with hers. She must see the cold call of death because her eyes widen before dropping to the knife in my hands.

"You are *not* the reason we are all in here. You never could be. You are merely a look-a-like. A poor replica of the original." I seethe watching confusion flash in her eyes as she backs up towards the wall.

"What do you mean? I got a note saying that I would survive the maze. That this was just a game to torture you all and I was merely here to witness it." she stutters slightly. Losing her confidence now that she is up against someone with similar traits.

"What are the odds you found a sociopath?" I grunt as my eyes tick to the camera hanging from higher up on the wall. They remain silent.

Figures.

"You will pay for that!" I speak louder and directly to them for the first time since I woke up in the maze.

Even though the speaker isn't on, I could swear I hear Basien's cackle.

I step towards her and a look crosses her face that I can't quite place, but it looks similar to acceptance. Good, because I won't show her any mercy. "How dare you think any of this could possibly be about you." I sneer, my anger ricocheting off the walls and doubling before it gets back to me. I swing the knife just like they taught me, the blade facing back towards my forearm as I swipe for her throat. Her arm comes up to block it and I end up slicing her arm instead. She hisses but moves toward me with more confidence than before. She drops her shoulders and tackles me to the floor. The hard concrete knocks the wind from my lungs.

"Bitch!" she snarls. "I have earned my freedom!" she screeches, like a howler monkey as she flails her arms, her inexperience causing her to flounder. Using that to my advantage, I turn my wrist and raise the knife over her side before slamming it in, the blade slides nicely between her ribs. I can hear when it hits her lung before her breathing changes and becomes shallow. Her eyes widen as she struggles, between the pain and lack of oxygen. I smile as I watch her. Her mouth gaping open like a fish as she fights to pull air into her deflated lungs. I twist the knife, making sure she feels every ounce of my anger.

Right before her eyes drift closed, slowly dying from lack of oxygen I pull her in close, my mouth level with her ear. "They are MINE!" I pull the blade from its snug spot in her ribs before bringing it back down over and over again, coating myself in a thick layer of blood.

Her body collapses on top of me, well and thoroughly dead. I lay there motionless as I draw deep breaths into my lungs, the feel of death comforting me. It's been so long since I've felt it.

As I lay there my mind travels back to the four years I've been trapped...an unwilling captive to the perverse puppeteers that control this whole thing.

"Better move faster than that, little girl." Bas laughs as *he shoves my back, forcing me to step forward and onto the shattered glass that lay at my feet.*

"Gotta be prepared for everything," Nox adds from where *he stands beside me with a stopwatch.* *"She'll move faster if she wants to eat tonight."* *I don't dare look at him but I can feel my jaw aching as I grind my back molars together. Every day they make me go through these stupid trials. They have been training me for something... what I have no clue. But I guess I should be grateful they are preparing me.*

"Move!" Bas *bellows, his deep smokers voice vibrating in my chest as my hands shake with fear.*

"I can't go any farther," I beg, struggling to not fall to the ground, knowing the glass would tear up my knees.

"Did I ask you what you could do, little girl? I said, Fucking. Move." I can feel his fury like a physical weight, forcing my legs to move even as the glass digs deeper into the souls of my feet. My weight working against me as the glass embeds itself through the muscle. I scream out as the pain becomes unbearable. My lungs struggling to take in oxygen and I can't seem to catch my breath.

"Please." I breathe.

The plead has barely passed my lips before I feel the back of his hand meet my face. My head whips to the side, my teeth clacking with the sear force of the blow.

"Don't be weak or we won't have any use for you." The man who took me from one cage and into the next, screams so loud in my face spittle flies out and lands on my lip. "I saw something in you that day... don't make me regret it." he finishes his voice only mildly softer.

"We will break you. The quicker you accept it the smoother this whole thing will go, little one." Nox adds, somehow with all his psychotic tendencies, he's gentler than his twin.

The thought of accepting any of this, causes my body to clench, everything tightening with the unnaturalness of it all. It's not the extreme training and running they force me to do. It's the killing. Every night before they offer me *food, my stomach wound tight and cramping with the lack of food that they dangle it in front of me. The smell of food wafting in from where ever the fuck they keep it teases me. The death of an innocent the preverbal bell in this Pavlovian conditioning. To meet my most basic of needs it costs someone their life. Their life or mine. And although I fought it and fought it for the first two months, they found other tactics of getting me to do it. They would give me an IV with fluids to keep me alive but would lock me in a pitch-black room for days on end. Torturing me in the most brutal ways imaginable. Making me wish and beg for a death that they would never grant me.*

It wasn't until they truly fractured my mind, it splintering into hundreds of pieces that I finally let go. Letting go of the girl my parents had mandated I be; forcing out the drilled in bible verses and unwritten laws of our rural community.

When they finally mended me, putting me back together like humpty dumpty after he fell off the wall. They didn't put the pieces back as they were, no, they put them back in the exact way they wanted. Molding me into the perfect woman for them. After four years I was finally ready– according to them.

This is what I was made for...

Chapter Eight

Nox

I watch her from behind the computer as she lies with the girl's limp body laying over hers like a sated lover. I smile smugly. I'm honestly surprised she was able to resist for so long. But she played her role well, and even had me convinced she cared about the girls.

I shake my head as my eyes shift to Bas's, his eyes are locked on her. He has always loved the sight of her in blood. Whether it was hers or someone else's, didn't matter. He likes to say I'm the sick fuck but when it comes to our girl he's willing to get fucking filthy.

As if answering my thoughts he says, "I can't wait to bury my fat cock in that tight little ass." he groans as he squeezes himself through his jeans. His long brown hair hung stringy around his eyes. He licks his full lips and I can't help but lick mine in response. We need to get our girl between us it's becoming too much to bear.

The fire that burns between us has always burned so brightly it's been hard to ignore, even more than the fact that we are blood related. Our whore of a mother was smart enough to at least get knocked up by the same man. I knew the night I met him at the house party my friends and I threw on the boarding school campus, that things would never be the same. Not because I had found my long lost twin brother, but because the sight of him made my dick so fucking hard there was only about half as much blood rushing to my brain. And I'd blame my boldness on that if anyone ever asked. But I caught him outside having a smoke, his lush lips pulled up in a smug grin like he knew everyone at the place wanted his dick. Girls and guys alike. No man had ever turned me on like Bas did. Fuck women barely turned me on the way Bas did, no one else but her. He must have seen it in my eyes that night because he quickly flicked his cigarette away before slamming me up against the wall. Staring deep into the silvery gray eyes that matched his and he said, 'Hello brother' as if there had been no doubt in his mind that we were related, then he planted his mouth against mine and didn't let up until I was begging for breath.

Drawing me from my musing, Bas says, "You think she's going to choose us?" The doubt in his voice is something I don't think I've ever heard before. He's always confident, mostly because he doesn't take no for an answer and just takes whatever he wants. I shrug my shoulders, not knowing the answer to that question.

"We will just have to give her no other option." I leer, taking a page out of his playbook. A menacing smile causes his sharpened teeth to peek through.

"Maybe it's time we chase our little psycho, what do you say lil' bro." he winks at me and my head tosses back as a laugh erupts from my throat. I'm up and heading towards the door without waiting for him. His deep laugh follows behind me and we make our way down the stairs and toward the maze.

"Ready or not, here we come!" Bas yells at the top of his lungs. I take out the X I had in a baggy in my pocket before popping one into my mouth. I grab Bas by the hair and tug his lips to mine before using my tongue to transfer the pill to him. His tongue fights mine for control before he takes it reluctantly, never wanting to be topped. He pulls back slightly and I hear him crunch on the pill before his hand frames my throat squeezing tight while tipping my head back. He uses his thick thumb to pry my lips apart before spitting the already dissolving pill back into my mouth. I accept it gladly before licking the bit of spit that clings to his bottom lip.

Then he reaches back into my pocket to grab another pill and take that one.

"We both know your bottom lil' bro. So stay in your lane." he growls, his hand still locked on my throat. I chuckle at the anger that shines in his eyes.

"Let's go get our girl." I finally say, not wanting to wait a minute longer to get balls deep inside her tight little cunt.

"You're lucky I love you or I would have already killed you," Bas mumbles to himself as he takes off toward the exit of the maze.

"ONE... TWO..." I sing.

"We're coming for you!" Bas finishes.

We enter the maze and I realize it's oddly silent, my eyes fly to Bas and he smirks. "Turned it off. Didn't want her getting hurt before we reach her." he winks and I shake my head.

"Now where's the fun in that?" I grumble.

"HA!" he mocks. "Like you want anything to keep you from that snug, warm pussy."

We take our time as we follow her, knowing there is nowhere she can go.

"You have a choice to make, little psycho," Bas yells to the seemingly empty space. "Your freedom or us...What'll it be?"

A growl threatens in my throat, not wanting to give her the option. She has been with us for four years, ever since Bas killed her family and took her from that Amish village. We trapped her in our basement, torturing her and molding her mind, bending it and fracturing it till she was just like us. Her mind, broken into dozens of pieces and forced to take on the shape we demanded. One that matched ours so perfectly that we knew we could never let her go. Our sweet little psycho had turned into the real deal.

She is perfect. Her innocence, still drawing others to her, her warm green eyes inviting and comforting, welcoming, drawing you in deep before she drops the mask and tilts her blade. God the sight of her covered in that girls' blood makes my cock so stiff it could hold up a shirt. I struggle slightly to walk with my dick plastered to my leg, I readjust it and Bas catches me.

"Thinking of our girl are we?" he teases as his eyes lock on my crotch.

"No, thinking of being balls deep in your ass." I bounce back and before I even see it coming his hand swings out and connects with my jaw. Fuck. His hand grips the back of my neck as he forces me to bend in half, my head level with his junk.

"I should make you eat my ass for that, but I think I'll wait." he nudges me forward and I smile like the cat that got the canary. Feeling like I got this win.

We pass the last few traps, avoiding the circular saw blades before we get to the piranhas. I reach for the long rope that's been tucked up high in the darkness on the wall. Freeing it to swing my way over the gap.

"How did our little psycho make it past this?" I question as I swing the rope back to Bas. He scratches at his beard as he contemplates, his head turning back toward where we just passed.

"Maybe she didn't?"

It's a heartbeat later that I feel her presence behind me. Before I can turn around the knife is plunged into my side. I know my little huntress missed anything of importance and that thought alone makes my balls draw up.

"Tsk tsk... Little one. You missed." I tease as I pull the blade free, bringing it to my lips to lick it clean with a moan of satisfaction.

"I meant to. Couldn't have you bleeding out before I got a chance to watch you gag on Bas's cock." she chuckles when she sees the look on my face and Bas bursts out laughing.

"See you're the bitch!" he points and laughs at me and I use the chance to catch him in the gut. The air is knocked from his lungs as it puffs through his lips, but his smile remains. I turn to our little one. Her eyes scream darkness and there is no sign of the soft, kind-hearted girl who was trapped in the maze. No, all that's left is our perfect little psycho.

My steps are slow as I approach her, but she just smirks as she backs away, always staying just out of reach. The second we are out from under the flood light she takes off, disappearing into the pitch black.

My hand goes to my side, feeling for the slit that's formed in my side, the blood tainting my shirt. "God damnit. I liked this shirt." I huff as I pull it over my head and toss it to the floor with a wet plop.

"Oh don't be a little bitch, Nox. We both know mommy and daddy's money will buy you a ton more." He mocks as he imitates my voice.

"And your mommy can buy you a new one too... oh, wait... that's right your mom was a crack whore who wanted nothing to do with you. Hmm..too bad." I jest back.

"You do realize we had the same mother right fucker?!"

"True, but I was wanted..." I raise a brow at him, waiting for him to refute it.

"You might have been wanted, but I got the bigger dick." he finishes cupping his dick in his large hand to emphasize his point before his shoulder plows into mine and he's walking past me towards our girl.

"Fuck you!" I spit as I follow, chasing after his laugh.

"Oh, we both know you can't take it, lil' bro." he says without turning toward me.

I hear Bas take a deep inhale before he lets loose a loud growl that seems to vibrate around the tight space.

"I can smell you, little one!" he roars, his voice taking on a deeper tone as his predator comes through. Bas has always been closer to his primal state than the rest of us. It's part of the reason he makes me so fucking hot.

Chapter Nine

Bas

I take deep breaths, my nose picking up the smell of copper and a distinct scent that is all Lenah.

I had always felt the desire to chase and hunt, but when I saw Lenah for the first time it was like someone flipped a switch in me, crossing all the wires inside me and making her my soul prey. No one or nothing else could fulfill my need like she did. I couldn't even wait to get back to the compound before I was balls deep in her virgin pussy. Stretching her to the point of tearing her. It's then I knew. I *knew* she was right for us. She didn't yell, she didn't scream, she welcomed the pain. Even as her blood coated my cock, slicking up her entrance and making my intrusion smoother, she thrived. The darkness within her growing. All it needed was a little nurturing, someone to show her her true potential, me and my brother were there to do just that.

My need to hunt her works its way through my blood, causing it to pulse to the beat of my throbbing cock. I will be balls deep within her and soon.

We move forward, moving faster with Nox at my back, allowing me to take the lead, knowing I need this. I close my eyes for a second, reaching deep, I know Lenny well enough to know how she thinks. So when we reach the next corner, one I know is a darkened dead end, I smile as I head down it.

"Where, oh where, could my little Len be..." I sing song as I know I'm getting closer. I snarl as I feel the slice of her blade cutting through the back of my calf. "Fuck." I grunt my body dropping slightly on the right side as my leg gives out. She springs out of her hiding spot, wrapping her legs around my waist as she causes me to fall onto my back, the blade now poised at my throat. "Whatcha gunna do with that, little psycho? You finally going to kill me?" I smile at her, my sharp teeth on full display, my heart thudding, knowing she is not only capable of doing it but the glint in her eyes tell me she is eager to. Her eyes drop from mine to my chest as she slides the sharp edge across my bare chest, my zip-up open and against the floor. I moan deep in my throat at the sting she inflicts. "Just another one for the collection love." I smile when she finally lifts the blade. My body is covered in tattooed scars, all of my pain not only on display but memorialized for all to see. I relish the thought of her mark permanently on my skin.

"My. Turn!" I thrust my hips causing her to flip off me as I transfer my weight on top of her, holding her down as my teeth sink into the fatty upper part of her huge tits. She moans and it's music to my ears, the taste of her sweet coppery goodness melting on my tongue. "This silly little scrap of a dress, teasing us with this juicy cunt. You thought I would let you!? You thought I would let anyone else see what rightfully belongs to me!" I bellow, my possessiveness breaking through. "You have been mine since the second I broke that tiny little pussy. Tore through that hyman and stole the last strip of your purity." I dig into my pants to pull out my thick shaft. Giving it a few strokes before tearing her dress free from her slight frame. Without any more talking, I slam my hips forward and bury myself to the hilt inside her. Feeling her wet warmth hugging my thick girth. The stretch causing her to release a slight hiss. I don't give her time to adjust. I grab her hips and pound into her, rocking back and forth so hard her teeth chatter.

"You will choose us. We may have given you the illusion of a choice but we aren't letting you go. Not now. Not EVER!" I emphasize my words with each punishing thrust. Her moans and mewls echoing off the rafters of the warehouse. I bask in the sound of slapping, as her breasts bounce off her ribcage. My eyes drift up to Nox who has his cock out and is stroking it to the sight of us.

"Like seeing your big brother balls deep in your girl?" I watch as his eyes flicker with heat. "Like watching my fat cock ruin her tiny little pussy?" I groan as my balls bounce off her round ass. Needing more, needing deeper, I flip her around so she's on her hands and knees on the cold concrete. I hear them scrape as I bury myself back inside her, but I don't give a fuck.

"Come on Nox. I think our girl needs something in her mouth." I encourage. Not needing any more influence, he steps forward and rips her hair back. She screams and I can feel her pussy tighten around my shaft as she shatters around my thick length.

"I will never choose you!" she yelps before Nox can get his cock between her fat lips. The rest of her protests are muffled by his length as he roughly fucks her throat. I don't stop my brutal attack on her cunt. That's the only description for what I'm doing to her poor body. I hear her gagging as me and Nox work in tandem, spit-roasting her.

"I won't last much longer brother!" I tell him as I work her so thoroughly I can feel her body stiffening beneath me as she fights to hold back her orgasm. I slap her ass as hard as I can, knowing the sting will light her up and push her over the edge. Her gurgled screams sound around Nox's dick and I feel his movements become more random as he loses his rhythm. "You going to cum for me, aren't you little brother? Choke her with your cum while your big brother dumps his load deep inside her raw hole." That's all it takes for Nox to grab the sides of her face and yank her down till her nose is smashed against his pubes and all nine inches of his thick cock are stuffed in her throat. She gags over and over again as she fights for air. Not letting up, he unloads all of his hot seed. Forcing her to swallow every goddamn drop.

"That's it little one. Suck his nuts dry." I purr as I reach around rubbing her overstimulated nub, barely finished with her last orgasm as I force her into another one. The tight grip taking me over and causing me to lose all control and I pull all the way out before slamming into her ass. She screams loud now at the sudden intrusion and the tearing it causes her but I don't give a fuck as I unload all I've got deep in her ass. Filling it so full it leaks out around me. Seeing an opportunity I reach for Nox, pulling him closer and forcing his head down to where my dick meets her ass. "Clean us up, lil' brother," I command, and he eagerly obliges as I pull myself out and he sucks my cum from her asshole. Blood and cum mixing on his lips as he goes feral for it.

"Fuck you taste so good together." he moans as he licks her from my cock, not caring one bit that it was just in her ass. He even licks her cream from my balls where it splattered there during her orgasms.

Wanting our girl to get as much pleasure as possible I lay on my back under her, burying my face between her swollen lips while Nox readjusts and straddles my cock, his pants removed as he lines me up with his tiny little hole. I groan as I feel him lower himself down on me.

"Fuck Bas, you're so fuckin' big," he grunts as he bottoms out. That's all he gets out before I'm thrusting up into him, bouncing him on my lap as I grab Lenah's ass and force her flush against my mouth, causing her legs to spread wider. "Yes...Yes..." Nox groans.

"That's right, take your big brother's fat cock deep in that tight little ass. You take me so well, Nox." I praise knowing he needs it before I bite and nip at Lenah.

"Bas...Bas...Bas..." Lenah whimpers as I feast on her, her taste driving me.

"So fucking good Lenah. You taste like Mine!" I roar as she reaches her peak once again and lifts slightly to spray me in her cum.

"More. Bas, I need more!" she screams as she vibrates with pleasure. I know exactly what she needs. And I will always give her everything she needs.

"Off!" I snap at Nox. He dismounts with a small pout as I force them both off me. "Lay down," I demand as Nox follows my command without being told twice. Lenah moans as I lift her and place her over Nox's raging boner, slamming her down, making sure she feels every one of his stiff inches. I lean her forward, sliding myself back in her ass. The immediate fullness causes her to explode, never able to take us both without creaming us both. "Good girl." I moan as I sink further inside her.

I moan, loving the feeling of Nox's cock rubbing up against mine, just a thin strip of flesh keeping our dicks apart. I know he loves it too because his eyes lock on mine and he winks. His hands roam her body, pinching and squeezing her lush breasts as they bounce for us.

"Fuck, how'd we get so lucky?" he whispers as he controls her thrusts with her breasts as my fingers indent in her hips with the force of my grip. We show her no mercy as we fuck her into oblivion, needing our release. On her upthrust, I slap her swollen clit before I command in her ear. "Cum for us."

"Nooo!" she screams even as her body follows my command. And I smile knowing she didn't want to come but her body obeys me.

"Yesss..." both me and Nox echo as we hold her down against us, forcing her to take everything we can give her.

"Gunna breed this tight little cunt!" Nox echoes my thoughts as we both nut inside her. By the time we finally catch our breath, she's dripping in semen. We both watch as it leaks from every hole, our smiles matching.

My hand finds her throat gripping it tight, watching as her eyelids lower and her breathing shallows.

"What's your choice, us or death?" I tell her and she makes a soft humming noise, a smile slowly growing on her face.

"Death," she whispers with the last bit of air in her chest. I growl as I squeeze tighter. Her eyes twinkle with mischief and I feel the tip of the blade. "Checkmate." she rasps as the point digs into my femoral artery beside my now rock-hard cock.

"Oh yeah, little one? We doing this again?" I fight back the smile of pride that I feel at her forcing my hand. Nox steps forward ready to interfere if need be.

I shake my head. My head tilts slightly as I study her, almost daring her to do it. "You won't make it out of this any other way, little one," I tell her honestly. I feel the blade dig deeper and my hand flashes out to grab it. catching her wrist before she can push it further. I pry it from her hand. Taking the hilt I shove it into her now gaping, thoroughly used pussy. "You think you could threaten me? Think I would ever let you go." my anger pours off of my words as I fuck her roughly with the handle.

"I wasn't asking for your permission." she snaps. And I smile, knowing it will just tick my little psycho off more. Nox needing in on the action crawls over her, licking the blood that's splashed across her gently tanned skin. He uses his teeth to get all the dried blood, leaving teeth streaks through the splotches painting her flesh in a pretty pink. His eyes drawn to where the knife is being sucked in, her pussy clenching around it.

"Silly little girl. You always need my permission. You don't breathe without my say so." To emphasize my words, my hand clenches tighter around her throat, completely cutting off her air.

"Is that all you got? And here I thought Nox was bottom." she taunts.

"Hey!" Nox yells "I am not bottom! Why does everyone think I'm the bottom!?" he huffs and we both
ignore him. The fucker pouts.

"Is this not enough for you, princess," I whisper,
my lips a breath away from hers. My eyes go to Nox
in a silent command, knowing my thoughts he leans
forward, mounting her face as he shoves himself in
her mouth, leaning forward to bite her clit, while I
keep my movements smooth with the knife. Handing
off the knife to Nox I circle around so I'm level with
his ass as he thrusts downward into her mouth. Her
hands grip at his sides as she tries to raise him off her.
Without giving either of them a heads up I fill Nox's
tight little hole to the brim with my cock, fucking his
ass while forcing him to fuck her face. "Come on little
bird, you know you will always be trapped within our
cage. Never to be free again." Nox moans as my hips
work his. His mouth full of pussy. I hear him slurping
and sucking as he gets into it.

I fuck them both so hard her body starts to thrash
as she fights for air that I won't allow her. "What's
wrong princess? Too much?" I prod. Her hips jerk and
she fights harder. "What? I thought you chose death. I
think this is a pretty way to go, no?" I sneer. Her hands
move to cover Nox's head as she forces him farther into
her weeping snatch. I hear him gurgle as she releases

and it squirts out, splashing against the concrete floor. The pitter-patter falling like raindrops.

Nox pulls back snorting and I know she sprayed him up the nose and he's struggling to breathe. I laugh at him as he struggles.

Chapter Ten

Lenah

My thoughts swirl looking for a way out of this. Nox's cock is so far in my throat I can't pull in any air and my vision is slowly fading around the edges, even as my climax builds higher than I think it's ever has before. The knife handle is still lodged inside me and I feel myself ripple around it as I creep closer to the edge, both to an orgasm and passing out. Just as my eyes sink closed and I feel myself slipping into darkness, Nox pulls out and slaps me across the face, shocking oxygen back into my lungs as I draw in a deep breath.

"Nuh-uh. You only die when we say so, little one." Nox says as he forces himself past my lips once more barely giving me enough time to fill my lungs once. My teeth graze down the sides of his thick shaft and he groans at the feel, enjoying my silent threat.

"Once you realize we control you, the easier this all will be." Bas finishes Nox's thought, and I can't help the anger that flourishes inside me. As much as my heart is now fed by them, the thought of them having that level of control eats away at me. They have had four years of my life to control me. They put me in this fucking maze, demanding I make it through to earn my freedom and I'd done just that, now I want it! I want it so desperately I can fucking taste it, and I will have it, even if it's at their expense. Eager to level the playing field, my knee comes up and connects with Nox's nose, I hear a sickening crunch as it shatters against my knee and he grunts.

"What the fuck Lenny! Not my Goddamn nose," he whines his voice nasally from his deviated septum. But he's backed up enough to free himself from my mouth and I'm able to slide out from under them before dislodging the knife from inside me and taking off running.

"You wanna hunt, big boy? Come fuckin' get me!" I scream into the emptiness, the infinite void of darkness. "You will never own me!" I keep going, my anger bleeding into my every movement. "You want a fuckin' toy you should have kept the other bitch." I don't even bother to hide my jealousy. Knowing the wall is up ahead, I launch myself at it, using my foot to propel me up. I grip the top before pulling myself over, knowing my lightweight and training for this is giving me an advantage. I drop myself over to the other side. This was where the long stretch was, so I head down the hall turning the direct one-eighty to the long dead-end hallway that we hadn't gone down the first time and hiding in the darkness. I crouch poised with the knife blade up and ready to attack. I can still feel their cum leaking from inside me, it drips down my thighs and I hear the soft patter of it hitting the concrete below where I'm crouched.

"You can play all you want, Lenny, we won't stop hunting you." Nox's voice sounds out before I hear a wad of spit hit the floor, no doubt laced with his blood.

"You belong to us, little psycho, you always have. You can fight this all you want but we will just hold on tighter." Bas states, his powerful voice rippling over me and causing my body to clench involuntarily at the knowledge of being owned by them, and that's how I know I have truly lost my mind. My need for them and the desire to get caught almost has me stepping out of the shadows.

But instead, I stay quiet knowing they are provoking me to fish out where I am. My fists clench in anger. I've earned my fucking freedom. I hear them huffing as they get over the high wall and land heavily on the other side, both of them being tall making it easier. I wait patiently for them to round the corner, my body wanting to pounce but I wait, making myself as small as possible.

"Left or straight?" Nox asks and I sense them pause, not being able to see them in the darkness.

"Both." Bas decides as he goes straight and Nox heads in my direction. I hold my breath as he passes.

"Come on out, love. We are only gonna hurt you a little." I can hear Nox's grin as he continues down the hall. I bite my lip hard enough to bleed, wanting to slice at his ankle but instead, I slip back around the corner and head back towards the wall and my escape. They think they have control. Time to learn a valuable lesson. I move on silent feet as I make my way back over the wall and through the maze. I still hear the boys calling out to me within the maze. At this point, they are getting angry and I struggle to keep my laugh inside.

Once I reach the exit I make my way to the stairs leading to the office and rush over to the command center Nox uses to control the maze. I flip the switch and turn everything back on.

I find the mask resting on the desk and slide it over my face before flipping on the TVs that are sprinkled through the maze.

"It's time to play a game," I say, my voice coming out feminine but distorted. "You want me that bad..." I pause for effect. "then you'll have to survive the maze."

I make sure I trigger every surprise he has, making it that much harder for them to get through. I sit and watch as they struggle to find their way through it. Nox has the upper hand, having designed it but as I flick off the floodlights even he's at a disadvantage. Plunged into pitch black, they fumble around getting injured by the traps. "You will earn your freedom with every drop of blood and shred of flesh. I will ensure it." I echo Nox's very words back to him through the speakers and I hear his grumble as continues running his hands down the walls.

"What do you want, baby girl?" Bas asks, his head tilted back towards the ceiling as he asks me. I lean back in the chair, contemplating how I want to play this.

"Will you even give me what I ask for if I set you free?" I suck at my teeth as I watch a sly smile flicker across Bas's face, knowing I caught on to him.

"As long as you ask for me to beat up that sweet little pussy of yours doll face." he rumbles, his chest rising and falling rapidly as the heat works its way through him. I smirk and clench my legs already needing the relief they promise. I close my eyes as a harsh, bitter laugh escapes me.

"I can get dick anywhere Bas, don't for a second think you're something special." my voice turns seductive as I push on his possessive nature, knowing it will piss him off the most.

"Ha! You and I both know ain't no one but me and Nox can fulfill your every filthy fucking desire. No one can match the depravity that we provide. Don't get confused sweetheart, we let you live that day I took you from your little poe-dunk village. Without us where would you be now? Married to some dude named Jaramiah and popping out his kids next to the rest of his six wives." I can see him roll his eyes. "Only fuckin' once you've showered and it's pitch black on the bed of organic cotton from your very own sheep. His little dick poking you as he fucks you missionary style. That could never be you Lenah. You have too much potential, potential we unleashed in you. It's us you need Lenah... Just as much as we need you." he finishes and my heart fractures, splitting off into two even pieces that only Bas and Nox could own.

I remain silent, waiting to see what Nox has to say. Bas chuckles and I know he seems to catch on to what I'm thinking.

"She's waiting on you Nox," he laughs as he nudges Nox's side. He purses his lips and I can tell he's trying to formulate a response but doesn't know how. Nox has always been more precision than action. He always left that to Bas. So we sit in silence, only the sounds of the blades and other traps whirling around us.

"I love you," he mumbles barely loud enough to hear and if I hadn't had the camera zoomed in on him and was able to read his lips I would have missed it. A smirk rises to my face.

"Awe, yeah, Nox? You Woooovvveeee me?" I can't help but tease him and I see his face turn into a scowl at my mocking.

"Fuck you, Lenny, now let us the fuck outta here." he huffs and I wait a few more minutes, letting them sweat but also because I don't want them to think I was listening to them.

"Fine. But only because I love you fuckers too." I share, "But you don't own me and the next time you shitheads think you do, I'll cut off your dicks and shove them up each other's asses. You got me?!" I say angrily, waiting for them to agree before I turn things off.

"Deal, little psycho." Bas moans, and I know he's stroking his thick shaft, loving me fighting back. He always loves when I put up a fight.

"Deal," Nox says begrudgingly and I flip the switch shutting it all down.

Epilogue

Nox

"Who do you think will make it this time?" I ask, my question directed at the little devil behind me.

"Well, honestly, I hope no one." she shrugs, not even bothering to watch the screen as the girls start to wake up. They all still look like her, but she has earned her freedom and us. My eyes slide to Bas who stands protectively behind her, his eyes dropping down her smooth neck and on the scar that she now bares there. His teeth forever marking her flesh, outlined in black ink like his.

I meet his eyes and we make a nonverbal agreement as he tugs her back against him. The black latex skirt she's wearing barely covers her sweet ass as he cups her bare pussy and grinds himself against her.

"You going to give us this sweet little pussy, doll face?" Bas rumbles in her ear, her eyes shuttering closed at the sound of his deep voice.

"Only if you've earned it." she grins, her eyes still closed. Knowing exactly what Bas is going to say, I drop to my knees and bury my face between her already soaking wet lips, letting her juices drip down my lips and over my chin. I stand quickly, gripping the back of Bas's hair and pulling his lips to mine.

"Tease our girl." I breathe against his lips seconds before my lips are plastered to his. Not one to be controlled, he yanks my head back forcing me to look at the ceiling as he licks her wetness off my lips and chin, making sure to clean up every drop before shoving my head back down.

"I didn't tell you, you could stop." I bark, holding my head down for good measure. Not that I would want to be anywhere else besides buried deep inside our little psycho's sweet little cunt. I quickly push her over the edge and keep going until she's screaming out for the second time, her body trembling as the sheer power of her climax overpowers her. Bas finally lets go of my head, allowing me to stand. I hear the buckle on his belt seconds before I hear his zipper and I know he's releasing that monster cock of his.

"Ohhh..." she moans as he sinks deep inside her. His arms sliding under her thighs before lifting, slaying her wide open for me.

"Join me, little brother." he purrs as he stays completely still, Lenah thrusting her hips, begging for him to move inside her. Not needing any more encouragement I yank my pants down and press myself against her already stretched pussy.

"You think you can handle both of us, little one?" I smirk, not allowing her to answer as I force my way inside her with Bas. Our cocks slide against one another and it forces a moan past my lips. I love the feel of her warm tightness against his sticky hardness, the contradicting feelings causing me to bite my lip to stave off the urge to blow my load right then and there. As if sensing my issue, Bas chuckles.

"Never pegged you for a two-pump chump, Noxy boy." Bas jest and if her pussy didn't feel so goddamn good I would punch him. My hands wrap around his sides and I see him grit his teeth as I drill into her, making him feel like I'm fucking him too. He shakes his head as he moves to take charge, never one to be outdone. Our cocks slide against each other as we rocket our girl into another orgasm.

"Fuck... Fuck!" she screams as she arches her back, her tits pressing into my chest as she lets go, her pussy squeezing our cocks so hard it hurts. Bas's jaw clenches as he fucks her ruthlessly, her pussy getting nice and red for us as he abuses it, her little nub swelling with her pleasure and I make sure I hit it with every thrust. Her moans turn into nonsensical words as she begs and pleads for us to make her cum again.

"Don't worry, doll face. We won't stop until you're making us good and fuckin' filthy." Bas nibbles on her ear before biting back into the spot on her neck, re-opening her wound and causing blood to drip over her full, bouncy boobs. I bite her nipple before licking up the blood, groaning at the taste of her. The added pain is enough to set her off again, but this time with direct contact with her G-spot. Bas pulls back on her hood, causing her to spray out all over my abs. Covering me completely.

"That's it baby, nice and fuckin' dirty." I moan at the warm feel of her cum dripping down all over my cock.

"I think it's only fair we get her a little dirty too, what'a think Nox?" Bas smirks. I nod taking her leg that he releases. I watch as he wraps his long, thick fingers around her throat, forcing her head back at an odd angle. Her eyes still half-mast, try to focus on him as a glob of spit drips from his lips and directly into her open and waiting mouth. Her deep moan causes my balls to draw up close to my taint. Needing to mark her the same way Bas has, I slap her big tit, causing them both to giggle before I spit, my eyes tracking it as it slides down her cleavage and rests in the dip of her belly button. The sight and feel of her slick juices coating my skin pushing me over the edge, sending me shooting rope after rope of sticky cum deep inside her and all over Bas's massive cock which is still buried inside her.

"Our filthy, dirty, little doll... Fuck!" Bas's head drops back and he pulses against my still hard shaft, which I refuse to pull out of this amazing cunt. I feel the warmth hit me a second later and I continue to work our girl, drawing out all of our orgasms as we rub against one another. Bas slowly releases her legs, holding her steady as she regains her balance. "You know, at this rate, one of us is bound to knock you up," he smirks as his eyes lock on her stomach. She rolls her eyes.

"Not if you didn't take my Goddamn birth control away." she huffs, but I don't sense any heat within it.

"But then how would we breed you, little one." Bas smirks, quite happy with himself. And I can't say I mind the image of her swollen belly, filled with our kid. She just shakes her head.

"Let's just watch the maze shall we." he plops down in my chair before I lift her and sit down myself, planting her ass on my lap. I place the purge mask on my face before clicking on the screen, making sure Lenny's out of the frame.

"Let the games begin..."

Trigger and Content Warning

Stalking

Kidnapping

Sadism

Blood-play

Hedonism

Incest

Drug use

Primal kink

Torture

Gore

Violence

Death of parents

Dub-Con

Non-Con

Spit-Play

DP

Taboo

Rough Sex

Breeding Kink

Murder

Rape/SA

Mentions of

Religion

MMF

DPP

Drugging

Acknowledgments

As always, I want to thank my girls, Ashley Trevino and Cheyanne Cruz. Who are not only Alpha readers, but also my editors. I love you girls to pieces and couldn't do this without you.

I want to thank my husband for his support and willingness to listing to all my crazy, outrageous ideas.

And lastly but certainly not least, I want to thank my reader because without you I wouldn't be able to do what I do.

If you enjoyed this book, please consider leaving a review as it helps indie authors like me so much. Thank you.

About the Author

E.R. Hendricks Is originally from Connecticut but now lives in Missouri with her husband and kids. She is a hot mess mom, to five kids and two fur babies. If she isn't reading books, she's writing them. Her hobbies include reading, writing, and COFFEE. She is new-ish to writing but truly loves it. She writes spicy romance and is even venturing into Horror. The tropes vary depending on her mood. She writes anything from fantasy/paranormal, contemporary, dark romance, in-sta-love, SyFy and more. The only limit is her twisted imagination. With a soft spot for psychotic men and strong, badass MFCs, you won't find any meek, frail women in her books. She hopes you enjoy her books as much as she enjoys writing them.

Also By E.R.

Out of the Shadows
Available on Kindle and KU no
Katerina is a funny, badass, ADHD having necro-
mancer/vampire hybrid.
She's sassy with a bit of crazy.
and when she finds herself at not only a new school but
an entirely new country, things are bound to go wrong.

Kiazer is a necromancer who is on the road to a suc-
cessful position as Dean of Runsfield Academy and a
committee member for the Supernatural community.
What happens when things aren't as they seem and his
whole world changes?
Will he change with it and go against everything he
knows for her?

**Out of the Shadows is the first book in a standalone
series with material that may be difficult for some

readers. This book has a HEA. It is recommended for 18+ due to language, sexual situations, and violence. If you like spicy this book is for you. Happy reading.**

The Pitch

Available on Kindle and KU now.

I'm in love with my best friend's brother.

Too bad the last time he saw me I was 14 and a dork.

Oh, and did I mention he plays for Manchester United, lives in Europe and dates models?

After a rough time in high school, I'm ready to start fresh.

When the chance to study abroad presents itself, I pounce.

With the change to get away and be closer to Aiden I can't pass this up.
The odds are stacked against me and the risk of losing my lifelong best friend.
Will Aiden finally see me, or will I continue to be just his sister's dorky best friend?

The Pitch is a novella with material that may be difficult for some readers, check trigger warnings. This book has a HEA. It is recommended for 18+ due to language and sexual situations. If you like spicy this book is for you. Happy reading.

<u>In Too Deep</u>
Available on Kindle and KU now.

The Mountain has always been my safe place, until it wasn't.

It was the place I went to escape from my mundane 9-5 desk job. My secret spot that allowed me to finally take a deep breath and clear my head.

It's where I escaped the darkness that always follows me.

I never thought it would all come crashing down around me.

Trapped with nowhere to go, I am forced to depend on the one man I promised myself I would never even speak to again, none-the-less depend on.

In too Deep is a novella with enemies to lovers, forced proximity, CEO/boss, age gap, and daddy kink tropes. This book has a HEA. It is recommended for 18+ due to language, sexual situations and violence. If you like spice this book is for you. Happy reading.

The Prince's Captive

Available on Kindle and KU now, under K.C. Gray

I'm trapped on a foreign planet millions of miles away from home.

He seems to think I'm his mate and therefore he has the right to me.

Well, he's got another thing coming.

I have babies and a life on Earth and I plan on doing whatever it takes to get back there.

She will be mine.

She thinks she can run, she thinks she can escape me, but she can't.

There is nowhere she can go that I won't follow.

She will help save us all.

The Prince's Captive is a novella and the first book in a Standalone Series called Alien Contact. This book has a HEA. It is recommended for 18+ due to language, explicit sexual situations, and violence. Please check TWs! If you like spice this book is for you. Happy reading.

Joker

Available on Kindle and KU now.

They made me who I am... Since I was a child the darkness has called to me, not just the darkness of night but the things that go bump in it. But now I am a thing that goes bump too. I am the thing they whisper about and hope they never see. I am not the boogeyman... I won't hide under your bed or in the closet. HAHAHAHA No... You won't see me coming but you'll feel me there. Her darkness matches mine.

I'm not sure why. Unused feelings turn in my gut stirring the cold, dark, shadows in my chest. But the shadows are where I belong, it's where I need to stay. It's where I hide my bodies. Will she be one of them?

This book contains material only appropriate for those 18 years of age or older. This book discusses mental health disorders and dark subject matter. This book contains profanity, explicit sex scenes, as well as various kinks including knife, blood, breath play, and other bodily fluid play. Degradation and praise are common themes in some of these scenes. This book will not be for everyone, it is dark, it is gritty, and it is based in trauma. If any of this sounds like it might not be for you, then please turn back now. Welcome to my madness!!

<u>Fated Moon</u>

Available on Kindle and KU now.

How did I get here?

Luna

My whole life has changed in a month and it all started with a gay ex-boyfriend.

After wasting three and a half years of my life with a guy who wished I had a penis, I find myself in a cabin in Quebec.

Thinking I would have some peace to get my life together...Nope.

Dash

I knew she was my mate the minute I scented her. Her intoxicating scent of vanilla and honey.

My wolf demanded I claim the little human as mine, but with my brother adamant that no wolf has ever mated a human, I was forced to put my feelings on hold.

That doesn't mean however that I would let my girl go. Hell No! She was mine and even if my dumb-ass brother didn't see it, I did.

Axel

Someone has to be the responsible one. Being the Alpha it's my responsibility to watch over my pack, even if my pack is just Dash now.

After he got us kicked out of our last pack, it's just been me and him for years.

We both desire mates and pups but at this point, it just doesn't seem possible for us.

There is no way Luna is our mate, I don't care how good she smells. No wolf would ever mate a human...

Fated Moon is a novella with Why Choose, Fated Mates, Age Gap, Grumpy/ Sunshine, Wolf shifter tropes and Primal Kink. This book has a HEA. It is recommended for 18+ due to language, explicit sexual situations, and violence. If you like spice this book is for you. Happy reading.

The Fighter

Available now on Kindle and KU

Kara Life hasn't always been easy, but I'll make do. I've got Benny and The Ring, that's all I really need. It isn't until dad gets into some deep shit that my whole life turns upside down. Now, I have to do more than just fight to survive, I have to fight for my life.

Alaric Being a fighter has always come naturally to me, so why not make money doing it? Fighting has been my sole focus for years. Until I see her... and all that changes. This girl will be mine, she just doesn't know it yet.

**This book's content and trigger warnings include violence, loss of a parent, addiction, and kidnapping.

This book is a novella with a HEA and a strong BA

MFC. It does have an Instalove/Insta-obsessed vibe. Thanks so much for reading my book and I hope you enjoy it!**

the Devil you know
Available now on Kindle and KU
They say the devil is in the details, but I think it's a lot more than that.
Running a billion-dollar company is hard enough but also making sure the sins are maintained is becoming... troublesome.
My business thrives on the sins of others, but when those pesky angels step in and start influencing miracles and sinning goes down I'm forced to handle things myself.

I won't let those feathered fucks stop me from achieving my ultimate goal. Especially him! He ruined my life once, I won't let him do it again.

I will have their sins and I will bask in the glory all the way to the top

They want to treat me like I'm the Devil, well then, you must give the Devil her due.

This book has a HEA. It is recommended for mature audiences only due to language, sexual situations, and violence. This book is on the darker side check TWS. This book contains BDSM so be mindful if that isn't something you enjoy. Happy reading.

The Evil Within

Available now on Kindle and KU

Camazotz

I'm drawn to the small town of Fort Gadsden, the blood calling to me like a beacon. But it's her that makes me stay. Her light, her innocence, her blood. She belongs to me, and soon... she will know it too.

Cecylia

I'm trapped in my home by my father, forced to participate in his sacrifices. A hopeless participant in his pursuit to serve his God. I don't know how much longer I can survive this, with each day that passes my hope dwindles. Until the monster in my shadows saves me. Now as I finally have my first taste of freedom, I'm forced to choose, do I escape his grasp, or do I surrender to my fate?

This book is a dark Monster Romance Novella. Please check Trigger and content Warning! This book is recommended for 18+ due to violence, and explicit sexual details. If you like a monster who looks like a monster and also has a few kinks and a knot, this book is for you!

Bloody Massacre Horror Anthology
Where Dead Things Lie
Will be released as a standalone novella.
When lust and murder meet, it turns into a devastating combination. Her past and present clash with her need to feed her insatiable desire. Trapped forever in her twisted game, where all dead things lie.

The Maze

These girls all have the same thing in common... they remind me of *her*. And for that, they will suffer. No one has ever made it out of my maze. I have designed it myself to be unbeatable, unpredictable, and unsurpassable. So, why do we do it, you ask? Well, isn't that obvious? We enjoy watching the mice as they try to find the cheese that is their freedom. The masters and they are the puppets. But what do we do when one of those puppets uses my maze to cut her strings? Will we give her the freedom she so rightfully deserves? Or will we keep her for ourselves...

The Maze is a Taboo, MMF Horror Erotica Romance. It contains dark themes and is only suitable for 18+, it contains graphic violence and gore. As always, there is a full list of TW and CW in my Bio's on all my Social Media pages and in the back of the book to avoid spoilers. Read at your own risk.

<u>This is the END</u>
Release Date-TBD
This can't be happening; this can't be real!
After the government "accidentally" released therapeía or the "Cure". I watched as the world and almost everyone in it changed.
A plague-like that of which the world has never seen
Running for our lives, me and my brother Luka, travel around the country to find a safe haven. But is anywhere really safe when 99% of the population is undead?

Forced to make a decision, I decided to leave my brother and travel on my own. That is until I find him...
Will he be my salvation or my downfall?

**This is the end is a post-apocalyptic/zombie romance, novella. This book has a HEA. It is recommended for 18+ due to language, explicit sexual situations, and violence. Please check TWs! If you like spice this book is for you. Happy reading. **

His Savior, Her Obsession
Release Date-TBD
At first, I watched him in a weird sense of protection, convincing myself that I was watching over him to keep him safe.

A way to pay it forward, but soon my protection turned
to possession and my paying it forward to obsession
I needed him to survive and not the other way around.
What will happen when he finds out?
My fear keeps me in the shadows where I am contented
to stay until I am forced to face the decisions I've made.
My only hope is that he won't run when he finds out
my secrets...

**His Savior, Her Obsession is a dark YA romance with
an older female/ younger male. This book has a HEA.
It is recommended for 18+ due to language, explicit
sexual situations, and violence. Check TWs! If you like
spice this book is for you. Happy reading. **

<u>Out of the Realm</u>
Release Date-TBD

I watch her from the shadows of the other realm.
She's become my deepest obsession.
I kill anyone who touches her
She is MINE, and I will not share.

I feel his energy when he's around
I feel his emptiness and his... urges.
But I'm up for a challenge, just like my plants, with a
little bit of TLC they always come back
I will save him from himself, or maybe he will drag me
to the other realm with him.

**Out of the Realm is the second book in The Runsfield
Academy Series. With material that may be difficult
for some readers. This book has a HEA. It is recommended for 18+ due to language, sexual situations with
explicit detail, and violence. Check TW! If you like
spicy books with morally gray, psychopathic Heroes
this book is for you. Happy reading.**

The Book Witch

Release Date-TBD

Have you ever wished you could spend time in your favorite book?

Have you ever wanted to go on wild adventures with your favorite characters?

Maybe have a book boyfriend you wouldn't mind visiting?

Cassie was living every book nerds dream at her book shop where the books call to her.

One-touch and a spell she can travel into any book she wants.

With a minute in the real world being a week within the book, she can have the best of both worlds.

Living in her apartment above the book shop, with her cat Binks (yes like Hocus Pocus) she is content to run her little shop and turn into an old bitty with a bunch of cats.

Determined to never fall in love after how her father left her mother.

Cassie prefers to live in the land of fiction, where there are happy endings.

But what happens when one of Cassie's adventures get a little too real and she falls for one of the characters within the book?

This book has a HEA. It is recommended for 18+ due to language, sexual situations with explicit detail, and violence. Happy reading.

Printed in Dunstable, United Kingdom